Th

Although Ann Cheetham has still to meet her first ghost she has always been interested in grisly tales. Once, on a school holiday in Belgium, she shocked the teachers by paying a secret return visit to an art gallery, to see a painting of a man being skinned alive.

She has lived all over Great Britain, and also in America, but her childhood was spent in Lancashire. Her architect father restored old buildings and she was lucky enough to live in several interesting houses, one with a mysterious "sealed room", another said to be haunted by a Civil War soldier.

Before family life took over she taught for several years and enjoyed it almost as much as writing. C. S. Lewis, one of her favourite authors, aimed to write the sort of books that he might have liked when he was young. She thinks this is a good rule to follow. Her first stories were written for her two sons, and they are her most valued critics.

Apart from books, she likes walking, cricket, listening to music, and singing—usually in the bath.

Ann Cheetham has written three other stories about Oliver and his cousins, Colin and Prill Blakeman: *Black Harvest*, *The Beggar's Curse* and *The Witch of Lagg*.

Black Harvest was picked by schoolchildren to be included in their twenty-four best books in the "Children's Choice" British book promotion of 1984. One reader said: "It was like opening the door of a fridge . . ."

Ann Cheetham

The Pit

An Armada Original

The Pit was first published
in the U.K. in Armada in 1987
by Fontana Paperbacks,
8 Grafton Street, London W1X 3LA.

Armada is an imprint of Fontana Paperbacks,
part of the Collins Publishing Group.

Printed in Great Britain by
William Collins Sons & Co. Ltd, Glasgow

for David

1948–1986

in loving memory

Take him, earth, for cherishing

'Ring o' ring o' roses
A pocket full of posies,
Atishoo, Atishoo,
We all fall down!'

Chapter One

Oliver Wright was walking home from the bus stop with his hands in his pockets and his eyes on the ground. You never knew what you might find in a London street. He'd picked a five pound note up once, all screwed up like an old sweet paper. He didn't get much pocket money, and even for that he had to do "jobs". That five pounds had been riches.

As he turned the corner into Thames Terrace a cold wind blew up suddenly from the river and made him prickle with cold. It felt like January, not June, and the coldest, wettest summer he could ever remember. July would be worse, August worse still because there'd be nothing to do, and no summer holiday. His father was in hospital, having a hip operation, and his mother was fully occupied, running the house like an army camp. He thought back wistfully to other holidays, several of which he'd spent with his cousins, Prill and Colin Blakeman. When those three got together odd and frightening things happened. Oliver and his curious "hunches" about spooks and hauntings usually started off as a bit of a joke, but he was the one who always got to the bottom of things, the one who always rooted out the reason for these strange adventures of theirs. Nothing interesting was going to happen this year though, not if he'd got to spend the summer all on his own.

The Wrights lived at Number Nine, the shabbiest house of all in a gloomy-looking old terrace. It was painted mud brown, and was full of old people, and it belonged to a special society that provided homes for the elderly. Oliver thought it was a ridiculous house for them to choose because it was so very tall and narrow, with fifty-seven stairs between the cellar and the attic. The old people never went down to the cellar, of course. It was infested with spiders and running with damp, and the attic was just a storage area, with one tiny bedroom for him.

He kicked gloomily at a stone and watched it bounce into the gutter. He liked their house with its views of the Thames and his bedroom under the roof, it was home. But on a wet Friday afternoon, with the whole weekend yawning drearily ahead, he wished there was another family in the street. Nobody lived there now, except the Wrights, and a few young trendies with their sports cars and their window boxes. The buildings opposite were old warehouses, shut up and abandoned, and at the bottom of their garden there was only the river. One end of the terrace looked out onto a little egg-shaped graveyard, neatly grassed over and raised up, almost two feet higher than the pavement. Its church, St Olave-le-Strand, had been pulled down last year, even though his mother had led the local campaign to save it. She enjoyed protests. Beyond the graveyard there was a demolition site filled with excavators and concrete mixers, and an enormous crane that swung an iron ball against crumbling walls and sent them tottering into dust. A huge warehouse was being pulled down and a new office development called River Reach built on the site. That would be something else for his mother to complain about. Why did she have to be so awkward?

Oliver was adopted, as Mrs Wright never failed to tell people. It was as if she thought they might ask difficult questions if she didn't explain – she looked rather too old to be the mother of such a young boy. He didn't much like the parents he'd landed with. Mother, with her iron-grey hair and wrinkled face, always so busy ruling Number

Nine, and Father, so silent and always buried in exercise books, peering out at him occasionally from behind thick glasses. They were kind enough, in a remote sort of way, but they weren't really tuned in to his world at all, and Oliver was lonely.

As he walked past Number Five he stopped to look at a black Porsche parked outside. It belonged to a young couple who had moved in last week. He smiled to himself. A car like that would mean parties, and doors banging in the middle of the night – another thing for his mother to complain about. He was just bending down to have a look through the window when a sudden noise at the end of the street jerked him upright again. It was a man's voice, shouting hysterically, then other voices and someone yelling "Hang on mate, for Gawd's sake, *wait* can't you!" Then, round the corner and running along past the graveyard, came somebody he knew quite well. Ted Hoskins, who worked on the demolition site.

Ted was over six feet tall, and beefy, and he wore very heavy boots, but he came tearing down past Oliver like a bat out of hell. His eyeballs were rolled up, right back into his head, horribly, like something dead, and there was an awful noise coming out of his mouth, half a groan, half a scream.

"Ted?" Oliver shouted, stepping into the street as two men from the site pelted past him, then "*Ted*!" He was always nice to Oliver, and he sometimes gave him things they found on the site. But now it was as if he'd gone both blind and deaf. He ran on, struggling to shake off the arms that clutched at him as the two younger men caught up, only stopping when he was brought down to his knees by a flying rugby tackle.

As Ted collapsed, and the two workmen bent over him, three more came hurtling along the pavement. Oliver crouched behind the Porsche, listening hard. He could hear the noise Ted was making quite clearly, and it chilled him. It was a moaning, sobbing noise, more like the helpless crying of a child than the voice of a grown man. He crept out from the car, stole along the pavement, and peered through a jungle of blue-denimed legs at the man lying in the middle of the road.

Ted Hoskins looked dead. His eyes were still open and staring, and his mouth had flopped open too, but the noises had stopped now and it was uncannily quiet. All Oliver could hear were the gulls mewing over the muddy river and, somewhere in the City, a muffled bell was ringing.

"Give him air," someone shouted. "The man needs air. Don't crowd him." Oliver recognized that voice at once. It was Rick, the bad-tempered foreman. He'd told him off several times, for hanging round the site. "I'm getting the boss," he said. "Throw a coat over him, somebody, and leave him where he is. We need a doctor for this. I'll go and phone."

As he turned round he almost fell over Oliver who was crowding round with the others, unable to take his eyes from Ted's face. "Clear off, can't you!" Rick yelled. "Can't you see the poor bloke's ill? Make yourself scarce, and quick, or you'll be in trouble. Now *get*!"

Oliver stood upright, and opened his mouth, but no words came out. He wanted to say he could help, that his mother was a trained nurse and that Rick could use their phone, but he couldn't speak. It was Ted's face. The look in those awful, rolled-up eyes had struck terror into him. Whatever had frightened the big kindly workman, down at the site, had stretched out a hand and was touching him too. Not just touching either, but plunging right down, down to the dark buried deep inside him, to the place where his worse fears were.

Everyone at school knew that Oliver Wright was a bit of

a weirdo, always borrowing other people's horror comics and taking them home to read in secret, always taking the creepiest books out of the library; and he'd never denied that he liked grisly things. What he felt now though was of a different order from all that. As he stared into Ted's face, he found himself remembering the worst moments of his life.

He remembered the day one of his mother's old ladies had died in her bedsitter, and how he'd seen the shiny coffin being carried down the stairs. He'd been told to stay in the flat that morning but he'd peeped, through the banisters, and he'd thought he'd heard the body, rolling about inside. Then he saw the damp cellar under the house, mouldy and reeking, where he was sometimes sent to look for jam jars, and he remembered the terrible day when his father had switched the light off, not knowing he was there, and how he'd been left all alone in the pitch dark, crawling about and unable to find the steps.

The look on Ted's face was about that darkness. As he stared at him, Oliver felt he'd been snatched away from the dull familiar street, with the rain falling and the knot of men still huddled in the road, plucked out of the dreary present and swept back, to the secret horrors and fears he struggled with at night, when the rest of the house slept. A deep silence enveloped him now, broken only by the curious, muffled tolling of that single bell. The very sound lapped him in darkness, and Oliver felt suffocated. Whatever had sent Ted Hoskins screaming down the street was here too, inside *him*. It was like a physical weight, dragging him down. "Did you hear me?" Rick was saying, and he shook him hard. "Do you want this boot in your backside?" But Oliver was already running, running away from the blackness, down the dingy street, not stopping till he was safe on his own doorstep, with the thin, cold rain dripping down his neck.

Chapter Two

He woke next morning to the sound of water drumming on the roof. He got out of bed and lifted up a corner of one curtain; the sky was the colour of pea soup. There'd been thunder in the night, followed by rain, the kind that set in with a vengeance then fell steadily, hour after hour. The demolition site would certainly be deserted this morning but it would also be a sea of mud. His mother might ask awkward questions if she saw him sliding off down the street, so he decided to postpone his visit to the site for a bit. It had been a bad night, full of horrible dreams about cellars and coffins. He didn't really feel up to tackling his mother.

On his way down to the kitchen, two floors below, he stopped on the narrow half-landing and looked through a front window. The sky looked several shades darker now, and it was still pouring down, but someone was out there, standing quite still on the opposite pavement, staring up at Number Nine.

Oliver pressed his nose to the glass and stared back. All the houses in Thames Terrace had tiny front gardens where nothing much grew, but theirs was special. Right in the middle was a massive oak tree, so wide that the front railings actually bulged out, over the pavement. It was supposed to be nearly four hundred years old, an "historic tree", according to Oliver's father, and there was a little bronze plaque on the trunk, telling you all about it.

Perhaps the person in the road was a tree expert. Oliver couldn't think of anything else interesting about their house. He stayed at the window, his pale cheeks flattened against the cold glass, and watched the figure move a few steps along the pavement. He could see it properly now.

It was an old man, very tall and spindly, with a lot of white hair blowing out from under a large black hat. He wore a very long black coat, black trousers and black shoes, and he was carrying a stick.

A funny cold feeling began to creep down Oliver's spine, and his dark dreams of the previous night started coming back again. This old man didn't belong to Thames Terrace at all; perhaps he was a ghost.

He shut his eyes tight and counted slowly to ten. When he opened them the tall black figure would have disappeared; flitted back to the world of make-believe, where it belonged. But when Oliver looked again the man was still there, pacing up and down the pavement, still looking up at the house, then down towards the little graveyard where the old people sometimes sat out on green benches.

Oliver watched him. Looking carefully both ways, and leaning on his stick, the gangly black figure crossed the road cautiously and disappeared into a green fuzz of leaves and branches. Seconds later there was a loud banging at the front door.

He peered down the stairwell and saw his mother come out of their kitchen. A smell of bacon and tomatoes wafted out with her. Muttering to herself, and wiping her hands on a tea-towel, she began to go down the stairs. Oliver followed silently, and stopped when he reached his usual vantage point, a little niche at the top of the first flight of steps where he could stay safely hidden behind a large plant stand.

The old man had a thin wavery voice but he spoke with a very refined accent. When he said "Good Morning" it sounded like a T.V. announcer, and he actually raised his hat. Oliver's mother would approve. She was always nagging him about good manners and good speech.

"I'd like one of your rooms," he was saying politely. "I

understand you have a vacancy. I've filled in the necessary papers, and I have my cheque all made out. How soon could I move in? I don't want to inconvenience you, of course . . ."

"Well, I don't know about this at all," Oliver's mother was saying, and she sounded distinctly annoyed. Raising his large black hat a second time, the old man had already walked past her, into the hall. He'd produced a sheaf of papers from inside his coat and he was fanning them out, under her nose. "The Society is quite happy for me to have the room," he said, "if you're in agreement, of course."

"Well, I'm not sure that I am, Mr – what did you say your name was?"

"I didn't. It's Verney. Thomas Verney."

"I have to explain, Mr Verney, that this is rather irregular, you see – "

"*Dr* Verney. Not a medical doctor, you understand, a Doctor of Science. I used to teach at the University. That's all behind me now, of course. I'm retired."

"I see."

Oliver peeped round the plant stand. His mother's voice had changed slightly. She'd put her glasses on now and she was inspecting the papers more carefully. He knew just what she was thinking, that a well-spoken retired professor from London University could give Number Nine a touch of class.

"As I say," Mrs Wright began again, handing back the papers, "the usual procedure is for a new resident to come along to the house *first*, with someone from the Society. The room may not be to your liking, you see, and in any case we may not get on with each other. It's a very small community, Dr Verney, and if people *don't* get on . . ."

"Oh, I'm sure I shall be very happy here," the old man interrupted, looking pointedly at the stairs. "I'm familiar with this street, you see, and I've always wanted to live here. So I wonder if you'd be so kind as to let me see the room?"

"As a matter of fact, it isn't quite ready," Oliver's mother said firmly, standing with her back to the staircase. "I've not quite finished dealing with the last resident's belongings."

The old man wasn't in the least put off. On the contrary, he started to ask a lot of questions about the house, questions which made him sound just a bit peculiar. He seemed obsessed with hygiene for one thing. Were there any rats or mice in the house, he wanted to know, with it being so near the Thames.

"*Rats*? I can assure you, Dr Verney," Mrs Wright informed him frostily, "I've seen nothing like that in this house, not in all the years I've lived here, and in any case, Mrs McDougall, one of my residents, has a cat. I don't care for cats myself, but they do deter rodents."

Oliver smiled to himself when he heard that. Mrs McDougall's Binkie was fat and spoiled. He wouldn't recognize a mouse if he saw one. And if he saw a rat he'd probably run a mile.

When he heard his mother coming up the stairs, with the old man behind her, he made himself scarce. As he let himself through their own front door he could still hear her going on about the empty room being "by no means ready", and about the Society's rules and regulations. So he was a bit surprised when she came up half an hour later and told him she'd given Dr Verney the room after all. "Well, if he settles in, it could be pleasant company for your father," she told him. "He's a nicely-spoken old man, highly educated of course, a real gentleman. It makes quite a change from Mr Porter."

"That wouldn't be difficult, would it?" Oliver grunted. Old Joe Porter occupied a large front room on the ground floor. He flew into violent rages when people failed to wipe the top of the sauce bottle, and he sometimes came home drunk from the pub. "When's he coming then?"

"Tomorrow. I explained about church but he said that Sunday was the only day his daughter could drive him here with his things. I told him not to arrive before 12. We'll be back by then. There won't be very much to carry in anyway, only the necessities. I've explained about the month's trial period . . . Dr Thomas Verney . . . I must write it down."

Thomas Verney. It sounded old. The boys at his school were called Kevin, Mark, and Lee, and they had surnames like Bates and Whittaker. The cold, creepy feeling he'd had, when he'd spotted the old man through the window, hadn't quite gone. Why on earth did he want to live at Number Nine anyway, with its fifty-seven stairs and its view of old warehouses? And how did he know there was an empty room? Oliver's mother hadn't told him.

Next day, as they walked back from church, the gang from the nearby flats were out in force as usual. Oliver always dreaded going past them. In two years' time he'd be at their school and if he hadn't grown a few inches by then . . .

The gang sniggered and made rude signs at his mother's shapeless brown hat. If only she knew how daft she looked, marching along with her Bible under one arm and his hand tucked firmly under the other. On seeing the gang Oliver shook free and pelted down Thames Terrace.

Dr Verney had already arrived at Number Nine, but there was no sign of his daughter, and no car. The front door was open and he was trying to pull a small tea-chest up the front steps, into the hall. It was crammed with books and it obviously weighed a ton.

"I thought we'd agreed that you should just bring the minimum, Dr Verney," Mrs Wright reminded him, eyeing the chest. Books were dust-traps, they'd got far too many in their own flat, and her new cleaner might object.

"But I must have my books around me, Mrs Wright." The old man was very polite but very firm. "Apart from those I've only got a small suitcase." And in two minutes he'd disappeared into his new bedsitter, and shut the door. They could hear him bumping around, then water running into a basin. "He's washing his hands already," thought Oliver. "He's obsessed with rats and mice, and keeping clean. He might have good manners and a posh voice, but underneath he's crazy."

His mother was still staring up at the first floor landing. She was lost for words – an unusual state for her.

"Shut the door will you, Oliver," she said, irritably. "It's blowing a gale in here. Some summer we're having; I wish it'd warm up a bit. There's no sign of his daughter, I don't suppose? I'd have liked a word with her."

Oliver went outside again and peered down the street. It was deserted apart from a young man in jeans and sneakers, lovingly washing the black Porsche; all its windows were open, and a radio was on full blast.

He put his hand on the door knob; he'd better get inside quick, or his mother would start complaining. Then he saw something. On the peeling mud-brown paint of their front door someone had daubed a bright red cross.

The paint was still wet and sticky, and running down the door in streaks. "What on earth," began his mother, coming out and seeing it. She looked down the street suspiciously, at the man cleaning his car, then she looked the other way, towards the Silk Merchant's house, the ancient, gabled shop that the tourists sometimes came to photograph. There were no signs of life at all, apart from rubbish blowing about and an empty Coke can rolling in the gutter.

"Well, we know who's responsible for *this*, don't we?" she said angrily, folding her arms and staring at the crude red cross, "and they won't get away with it either."

"Who?" said Oliver.

"Those louts from the flats, of course. They must have done it while we were out at church. I'm going inside to phone the police. They'll sort them out. It's an absolute disgrace."

Oliver lay awake for hours that night. Every time he drifted towards sleep his muddled, troubled thoughts tugged him back to consciousness. He was getting frightened. First Ted Hoskins appeared to have gone off his head, and had run screaming down their street, then this peculiar old man had turned up out of the blue. Now some yobbos had daubed their house with red paint. Oliver didn't like it at all. His mother was always nagging him, about the creepy books he read, and about his curious obsession with grisly things. "You can have too *much* imagination, Oliver," she was always telling him. But it wasn't "imagination"; he knew something was wrong.

The police had interviewed the gang at the flats and they'd denied everything. "Well, they would, wouldn't they?" his mother had informed the young sergeant. "Of course they did it, it sticks out a mile."

"But why paint a *cross*, Mrs Wright?" the man had said nervously.

"Because we're churchgoers, of course. They're always on the streets when my son and I go to morning service."

His mother was going to scrape the front door first thing tomorrow morning. But Oliver was haunted with the idea that she would never actually manage to get the paint off. However hard she rubbed, that awful red cross would stay.

He drifted into unconsciousness at last with the sound

of a muffled bell tolling in his head. That was odd too, because it sounded quite near. The only church he knew of round here was St Olave-le-Strand, and they'd pulled that down months ago.

Chapter Three

He set off for school early next day because he wanted to call in at the demolition site on the way to the bus. His mother was already busy on the front door, hacking away viciously with a rusty old scraper from his father's toolbox. She'd got all the red paint off but the cross still showed through. It was a sandy-white now, because she'd scraped down to bare wood.

"The Society will just have to get it repainted," she said. "They can't put it off any longer." Oliver slid off while she was still talking. At least the awful red cross had gone and the weather had improved too; it was actually quite warm. As he walked down the sunlit street, his fears of last night seemed slightly ridiculous. Perhaps Dr Verney was just an ordinary old man; all his mother's residents had their odd little ways.

At the site, most of the men were in T-shirts, and a few had stripped to the waist. Oliver stood by a huge pile of rusty pipes and watched them working. After making sure that the foreman wasn't anywhere around, he walked over to Geoff Lucas, one of his favourites. The whole site was marked off into sections by posts strung together with lengths of orange tape. "Is this where you are going to start excavating?" he asked Geoff, secretly admiring his suntan, and his big rippling muscles. Why did he have to be so puny and small? Why couldn't he *grow*?

"That's right," Geoff said, rubbing the sweat off his face and leaving a great smudge across one cheek. "When you put up a building as big as this the foundations have got to go down deep. We won't be starting on the footings yet, though. We've got to clear all this rubbish first."

"But I thought you'd already started. What are those big

holes everywhere?" He could see quite a few places where the soil went down several feet. They looked like moon craters except that they were square, not round. He'd thought those were the new foundations.

"Those were cellars, under the old warehouse. We've been taking old drainpipes out of those. Ted Hoskins was working on the job when – "

"When he was taken ill?" Oliver's heart gave a queer flip and he stared hard at Geoff Lucas. "He was ill, wasn't he?" he went on, when he got no answer.

"Dunno mate. Don't ask me." The man bent over his spade and started to scrape thick gooey mud off it with his boot – he'd begun whistling tunelessly.

Oliver was quite determined to find out what had happened to Ted Hoskins, and he stood over Geoff while he worked, firing off a battery of questions. "Look, mate," the man said at last, throwing down his spade, "all I know is that he went running out of this place. Perhaps he just needed the bog or something. I mean, I dunno, do I? Anyway, he's off sick today. Go and ask him what's up, if you're so interested."

"Do you know where he lives?"

"At the flats. It's only a stone's throw. The caretaker'll give you the number."

"The flats" was bad news for Oliver. Going there might mean being seen by that gang. But he was definitely going to visit Ted after school, gang or no gang.

He decided on a change of tack; it was no good irritating Geoff. He might turn nasty, like Rick. "Found anything interesting lately?" he said, more casually. At home he'd got a very old penny that Geoff had given him, and two pieces of white tubing that his father said were bits of old clay pipes. Geoff felt in his pocket. "Well, there's this. I picked it up on Friday . . . Not sure I'm going to give it to you, though. You're a bit of a nosy parker, you are."

"Go on, Geoff. What is it?"
"How do I know? You tell me."
Oliver took it and held it at arm's length. It was a small, insignificant-looking stone, smooth and black, like something you might pick up on a beach, but it was shaped like a rough triangle, not an egg, and at the narrow end there was a hole bored right through.
"There are some marks on it," Geoff said, fishing in his pocket for a packet of cigarettes, and lighting up. "Can't read them. I bet your Dad'd know what it was."
"He's in hospital," Oliver told him. "He's just had a big operation on his hip. I could show it to him though." He held the stone up to the light and squinted at it. If the marks were letters he certainly couldn't read them. He'd need quite a powerful magnifying glass to do that. "The hole's odd," he said thoughtfully. "Perhaps it used to have a string through it. Perhaps someone wore it, you know, like a necklace."
Geoff sucked on his cigarette and pulled a face. "Not very pretty though, is it? Why wear a thing like that round your neck, for Gawd's sake?"
"Can I have it?"
Geoff nodded. "O.K. But don't say I never give you anything. And I'd keep out of Rick's way if I were you. He's in a bad mood this morning."
"He's always in a bad mood," Oliver said, slipping the little black stone into his pocket and slinging his bag of books on to his back again.

The minute Oliver walked into the playground a girl called Tracey Bell waddled over to talk to him. She'd obviously been waiting for him to show up. People laughed at Tracey behind her back because she was very short and very fat. She wasn't at all pretty and she had a frizz of blonde hair the texture of pan scrubbers; she was no good at school work either.

Oliver felt a bit sorry for her. Lessons were no problem for him, he was always near the top, but he knew how it felt to be "different". He was odd to look at too, with a large head that looked much too big for the scraggy neck that supported it and pale, rather bulgy eyes; and he was the smallest, weediest boy in the whole class. He was no good at games either, even worse than Tracey Bell. People called him a wally.

Tracey didn't have a dad but everyone knew Mrs Bell. She was just a bigger version of her daughter, with the same kind of pan-scrubber hair. "I might be coming to your house this week," she told Oliver excitedly. "My mum's doing a cleaning job for your mum. Good, i'n't it?"

Oliver stared at her round moon face; he could have kicked himself. He'd told Tracey last week that his mother was looking for a cleaner, but he'd never imagined that she'd tell her mother, or that Mrs Bell would knock on the door and ask for the job.

The news put him in a bad mood. In spite of his secret sympathy for Tracey, he felt threatened, afraid that she might start poking and prying. She'd ask him why they hadn't got a television and why he always had to go to bed so early, and why his parents were so old.

At nine o'clock he filed miserably into the school hall with the others, all set for a depressing week. Most lessons bored Oliver because he was so clever; he always finished first then he had hours to kill. He usually ended up messing with the things in his desk, then he got told off, or sent to the library for "private study". That was boring too, because he'd read all the books that interested him.

But after assembly something quite exciting happened. The science master stood up and told them that their school, Dean Street Middle, had been chosen as the main location for a new television project. Kit McKenzie, the famous T.V. "animal lady", wanted to come to the school and film *them*. It wouldn't be lions and tigers, it'd be domestic animals, ones you could keep at home. But she was on the lookout for something unusual. "If you've got an interesting pet at home, or can get one," the science master told them, "find out all about it, make notes on the way it behaves, what it eats, all that sort of thing. You never know, you might be one of the lucky ones and end up on television."

At break everyone was talking about the animal project. Most people had pets like mice and hamsters but one boy had a lot of stick insects and a girl in 3.B. said she was going to borrow a parrot from her Grandad and Grandma. "It can sing pop songs," she told everybody, "and it swears."

"I don't think they'd want that on T.V." Tracey Bell said, in her loud, penetrating voice, sidling up to Oliver.

He was feeling rather depressed as he listened to all the talk about gerbils and Siamese cats, and about a large spider called Boris that had lived for two years in William Briggs' bathroom cupboard. His mother would never let *him* have a pet, not even for something "educational"; she made enough fuss about Binkie. There was no way he'd get on T.V. Then Tracey sprang a surprise. "My Uncle Len's got a pet shop," she whispered, cornering him in the playground by the bike racks. "He could get us something interesting."

"*Us*?" Oliver repeated suspiciously.

"Well, we could do our project together, couldn't we? It'd give us a lot more chance."

It was Tracey Bell's dream to go on television, and she'd got it all worked out. Oliver was the cleverest boy in the school so he could do all the writing and reading up, and her Uncle Len would get them the animal, something a bit different, if she wheedled him. They just couldn't lose. "What sort of thing do you fancy, Oliver?" she said brightly. It was hard to crush Tracey Bell.

Oliver didn't fancy anything, and he didn't fancy appearing on the T.V. screen next to her. They'd look ridiculous, like Little and Large. "A rat," he said stonily. That might shut her up.

"A *rat*? Ugh . . . *Oliver*. What do you want one of them for?"

He didn't know, he'd just said the first thing that had come into his head, though he must have been thinking about rats anyway, because of all Dr Verney's questions about rats and mice.

"Well, at least it'd be something different," he told Tracey, feeling a bit mean. Surely her Uncle Len didn't sell rats in his shop? He'd never actually heard of anyone keeping a rat as a pet. Though now he actually thought about it, studying rat behaviour might be quite interesting. Weren't they supposed to be highly intelligent? He dimly remembered reading a book once, a science fiction story in which rats had taken over the world.

"If Uncle Len *can* get us anything it'll have to come to your house," Tracey told him. "We live in a flat and we've only got a balcony. My mum won't let us keep anything out there."

Oliver didn't reply. Tracey's uncle would probably say no, for a start, and if he did come up with anything he couldn't see his mother letting him have it at Nine, Thames Terrace. As for keeping a rat . . . he could just see her face if he came home with one. It was such an awful thought it was almost funny.

Chapter Four

He found Ted in a stuffy room, sprawled in a chair, staring listlessly at a T.V. set. It was on low and the news commentary was hardly a mumble, he couldn't be listening. And he wasn't looking at the screen either, his eyes were going straight past it.

"I've brought you a present," Oliver said, holding a paper bag out. Ted took it and looked inside. It was a chocolate bar, fruit and nut, the kind he sometimes brought in his lunch box. Oliver knew he liked it.

"Thanks, pal." But the man didn't eat it, he just carried on staring at the television. The voice didn't sound like Ted's, and the face wasn't Ted's either. It looked too white and shocked, and the eyes were still fish-like and glassy. "What's up?" said Oliver, sitting down next to him, on a red leather pouffe.

There was a long silence. "Are you coming back to work soon?" Oliver tried again. He was looking at the man's large, square hands, lying idly in his lap, at the kindly, weather-beaten face and the scanty fringe of greying hair round the speckled, bald head. He was fond of Ted Hoskins, and he'd decided that if he ever had a serious problem he'd go to Ted with it. In fact, he sometimes pretended that Ted was his real dad. It was awful, with his own father in hospital.

"No, I'm not, son. I'm not going back there. They can give me my cards if they want. I'm not bothered." His voice was colourless and flat, as if all the stuffing had been knocked out of him, and Oliver felt little prickles going up and down his back. The neat sitting room, with its hard, bright colours, seemed to fade into a dull blur. Something else was taking its place, a harsh cold breath, like the first nip of winter. It was in his brain and it was inside him, squeezing out all the warmth and the light, all the ordinary, reassuring things.

"What exactly happened, Ted?" he could hear himself saying. "Did you find anything? I mean, at the *site*?" But Ted's wife had suddenly materialized from the kitchenette. She'd gripped Oliver firmly by the arm and was now steering him out of the room. He tried hard to resist. He'd not even started his investigations yet.

"But I want – " he began.

"He didn't find anything, duckie, nothing at all. He just came over a bit queer, that's all. He's got high blood pressure, you know."

"But it was worse than that, Mrs Hoskins," Oliver said doggedly, a helpless feeling coming over him as he saw the living room door shut on Ted. "Something really awful must have happened. I mean they must have dug something up, something nasty. I saw the look on his face."

The plump little woman in the blue overall looked at him thoughtfully. She'd never met a child like this before. He seemed so old, so knowing and he had such staring eyes. Well he wasn't going to upset her Ted with his questions. "They didn't find anything," she told him. "Ask one of the others if you don't believe me. It's true."

"Well, what did happen then? Why did he run away? He *did* run away, I saw him."

She hesitated. He wasn't going to leave unless she told him a bit more; he was obviously that sort of kid. "He said . . . he said it went all black like," she began slowly, "all *dark*. Very dark and . . . thick, you know, *foggy* . . . oh, I don't know, duckie. Life's a funny thing."

She felt very embarrassed. She'd told Oliver exactly what Ted had told her, and she still couldn't make head nor tail of it. She opened the front door pointedly, and waited for him to go through.

But Oliver didn't budge. "*What* went all black?" he repeated, in his high, penetrating voice. "Did he *see* something? That's what I want to know. What frightened him?"

"I've told you, he just came over a bit muzzy. He'd probably forgotten to take his pills."

"Well, if that's all it was why won't he go back?" demanded Oliver, "and why did they get an ambulance?"

"Look, love, it was nice of you to come and that, but I don't want him upset. Off you go now, he might be back at work next week." And she shut the door on him.

Oliver stood outside on the landing, staring at Number 16. He felt like kicking the door in. It was quite obvious that Mrs Hoskins knew things she wouldn't tell; it was probably in the hands of the police by now. All she'd wanted was to get him out of the flat. He turned away angrily, and started to go down the chilly staircase. Why did grown-ups treat children like idiots?

But he was wrong about Mrs Hoskins. She'd been unnerved when they'd brought her Ted home in that ambulance. He hadn't been able to tell her what he'd seen, but it must have been bad because he'd threatened to give his notice in.

Oliver thought about Ted all the way home. He simply didn't believe what Mrs Hoskins had said about the pills; Ted's face had told him the truth. Perhaps they'd not actually dug anything up at the site, but they must have disturbed something.

It was as if a great black bird was on the wing, flinging a cold dark shadow across London, changing the way everything felt, changing him. "Blackness and darkness", that's what Mrs Hoskins had talked about, in her tight, embarrassed voice, not understanding. He'd felt that darkness himself, out in the street, peering down at Ted's face. He'd *felt*, but he'd not *understood*. And he still didn't understand, not properly. Big beefy Ted, always whistling and cracking jokes. What on earth *had* happened, at River Reach?

After tea Oliver slipped down to the cellar. Mrs Wright had bought a lot of plums and she was planning to make jam. He'd offered to go down and find new jam jars for her. It was a good move because he wanted to have a good look round, but he didn't want to make her suspicious.

As he went past Dr Verney's door he heard raised voices. His mother was in there, talking to him, and she sounded annoyed. "I can assure you, Dr Verney," she was saying irritably, "there is nothing like that in this house, and, if there were, Mrs McDougall has a cat. Now you really must stop worrying like this . . ." He must be going on about rats and mice again, Oliver decided. He was nuts. He felt rather uncomfortable as he made his way down the cellar steps. If only Dr Verney knew what he and Tracey Bell were hatching up between them.

If Uncle Len did produce a rat for them, it would have to go in the cellar of Number Nine. It wouldn't mind the dark, and Oliver was planning to put the cage against the front wall, where there was an iron grating, and where you could peer through a little cobwebby window and look up into the street. The thing was to keep it a secret from his mother. If the rat behaved itself, and they got on well with the project, the time may come when he could risk telling her. But even though she hardly ever came down to the cellar it was vital to keep the rat out of sight.

Fortunately that would be fairly easy. There was rubbish of all kinds heaped up round him, boxes and crates, and discarded doors, and sagging piles of yellow newspapers. And since the cellar was much too damp to be of any practical use, it was just a place for jam jars and paint cans, for large hairy spiders and now . . . *rats*.

It was large, occupying as much floor space as the house above. Oliver crept about in the dim light, trying not to bump into things. He couldn't spend too long down here, he'd only come for jam jars, and if he didn't go upstairs soon his mother would appear and fetch him out. She didn't like his habit of "grubbing around".

He ran his fingers over the damp walls, under the flaky white paint; they were all knobbled and bumpy. It didn't feel like bricks at all, more like big pebbles, all flung together. His father had told him that this part of the house was centuries old, that there'd been at least two houses built and pulled down on top of it. He couldn't get down here any more, because of his bad hip.

Oliver wandered about, putting dusty jars in a box, and trying to decide on the best place for the rat. Then he saw them, not skulls or rolled-up documents or heaps of gold coins, but *cracks*, dozens of little cracks running down the wall from top to bottom, on the left side of the iron grating.

He stared hard, put his face close to the greenish, cheese-smelling wall, and examined them carefully, sticking a finger in. They were new, he could see bits of plaster on the floor, plaster that must have fallen out of the cracks. So his mother was right after all. She'd been up in arms from the beginning about the lorries from the building site rumbling past the house at all hours, and about the huge trailers dragging heavy equipment. She'd said it would shake the old house to its foundations, and it had. These cracks were living proof.

She'd be pleased about the damage in one way, at least these cracks proved she'd been right to complain. A couple of them were quite big, almost big enough to get your hand in. He leaned forward cautiously, and sniffed. A cold sooty smell came out of the holes but he couldn't see anything. Next time he was down here he'd bring his torch and examine everything properly.

"Oliver? *Oliver*!" He scuttled round, putting a few more jam jars into his cardboard box, and wedged it under one arm. He needed a free hand to negotiate those stone steps, he'd really hurt himself if he fell backwards, with a load of broken glass on top of him. "OLIVER!!" His mother wasn't very patient, she'd finished sorting out Dr Verney and now she wanted to make a start on her plum jam.

But her high, piercing voice was suddenly drowned by a terrific noise up in the street; a great yellow machine was being dragged past, on its way to the building site. He could hear the rumble of enormous wheels and an orange light was flashing through the bars of the grating. As it rolled past, the house over his head seemed to rock slightly, the naked light bulb shook on its flex, and a lump of plaster suddenly detached itself from the sagging ceiling, hitting him on the shoulder as it fell to the floor.

"OLIVER!!" She was getting really angry now, but the boy took no notice. He put his box at the foot of the cellar steps and made his way back towards the grating, groping as he crossed the dusty floor. The dangling bulb seemed much dimmer, in fact he could hardly see, and the sun wasn't filtering down through the grating. It had gone quite dark outside.

He stood quite still, with his hands in his pockets, one little finger playing with the hole in his stone, the stone with the marks on that Geoff had given him. Slowly he ran his eyes over the ceiling; now he looked more carefully he could see several places where large pieces had fallen off, and there was rubble on the floor, and on the bundles of *News Chronicles*.

Oliver listened. At least his mother had stopped yelling. She'd have gone up to their flat to look for him. But someone was in the hall – or was it outside? He could hear a voice, rather faint, but getting clearer, a woman's voice, gentle and young, and she was crying.

He glanced up through the grating but there was nobody in the street outside. Then he turned round; whoever it was must surely be standing very close to him. But there was nobody there. Oliver's stomach lurched, and a cold icy feeling swept over him. Every inch of his scalp tingled, as if he'd been stripped naked and plunged into freezing water.

Slowly, unable to stop one foot moving ahead of the other, he moved steadily towards the grating. Then he found himself gliding sideways towards those long dark streaks in the wall, and one of them was opening up, like the earth cracking, like a huge mouth. Out of it came a roaring, terrible blackness, sweeping round him and over him, stopping his breath.

And Oliver let himself be taken, soundlessly, without struggle; the only noise in the cellar was the woman's voice, that desperate, anguished weeping that went on and on, losing its gentleness and turning strident and hard until, at last, it became one ear-splitting agonized scream.

Oliver passed into nothing. It was as though his own head had grown huge and split open silently, and as if all the darkness inside had flowed out like a great river, choking him, and swallowing him up.

Chapter Five

He was looking out of a dirty window, down into a street, standing on tiptoe because his chin barely reached the sill. He wore a greasy brown tunic with a leather belt round the middle. His feet were bare and, between his toes, he could feel grit and dirt from the wooden floor.

It was suffocatingly hot and the small square of sky outside was a flat, hard blue. But worse than the heat was the overpowering smell, and Oliver was trying to snatch quick light breaths of air. If he took proper lungfuls he knew he'd be sick. He tried to analyse the smell but he couldn't. One minute it reminded him of meat that had gone bad, the next of a huge manure heap. But farm smells could be quite pleasant in a funny sort of way. This wasn't, it was a smell of rot and decay, not just hanging in the air he breathed but somehow in his own body.

He looked down. His hands and feet seemed curiously small and they were filthy, every inch of skin uniformly grey. His mouth tasted foul, his teeth sticky, as if he'd not brushed them for years and years.

He pushed his face up against the window, rubbed a little hole in the dirt, and looked through again. There were houses opposite, half-timbered with sagging tiled roofs, and with upper storeys that stuck out over a cobbled street. They were so close he could have leaned out and shaken hands with someone opposite, if there'd been anyone at home. But the house looked shut up and deserted, so did the houses to the right and left, and up through the egg-shaped cobbles he could see grass growing in little tufts.

He must be in a town because there were roofs and gables and chimneys, stretching away till they dissolved into a brown-red blur under the heartless blue sky. But it felt like a town of ghosts. Nobody came or went in that narrow little street, nobody called out. The only sound he could hear was a bird twittering away in the leaves of a fresh young tree that was growing up, just under the window.

Oliver craned his neck till he could see right along the street and spotted something he recognized, a different sort of house, more like a shop. He thought he saw a figure moving about behind the upper windows but the lower part was all boarded up, as if they were going to pull it down. The street door was a faded green colour, studded with diamond-headed nails, like the entrance to a dungeon, and painted on it, in broad rough strokes, was a bright red cross.

As he stared he saw a figure pass in front of the houses opposite, walk down to the "shop" and take up a position outside the peeling green door. It was an old man, quite bent, with a straggly beard. He wore a peculiar cone-shaped hat and faded knee breeches and, in spite of the heat, he had a cloak wrapped round him, dark red, the colour of plums.

Oliver saw him put something down on the cobbles. It was an old-fashioned lantern, the kind that took candles; he'd only ever seen them in books. The man looked up at the house then peered vaguely along the street. No one moved, no one spoke, there was only the bird, singing its heart out in the pale green leaves of the little oak tree.

Then he picked up a pole that had been leaning against a wall. It was a pike. Oliver could see the sun flashing on the big curved blade as the old man hobbled up and down. He took six steps up the street, then six back. Then he leaned against the shop and closed his eyes for a minute.

before setting off again. He was obviously doing some kind of sentry duty, as if it was his job to make sure the people inside didn't escape. But *why*? That house looked ready for the demolition squad.

He watched the man take a couple more turns up and down the street, then he dropped away from the window. His feet were aching after standing on his toes for so long so he turned round to see what was behind him.

Precious little. A dark room that smelt nearly as foul as the air blowing through the gap in the window frame; low box-like beds, each one a tumble of blankets. There were no pictures, no shelves with ornaments, no books, and the floor was bare except for a dented tankard lying on its side, and a tin plate scattered with crumbs.

Oliver could hear muffled voices. He spotted a little door in the far corner and began to tiptoe across the floor, grit sticking to the soles of his feet like spilt sugar. Then he stopped dead. Something was moving by one of the beds, creeping across the floor in and out of the dusty shadows. Something sleek and black with quivering whiskers; it was a rat.

He shrank away, watching open-mouthed as it found the plate, ate the mouldy crumbs delicately, taking its time, then sat on its tiny haunches, dabbing at its face like a miniature cat. Oliver clapped his hands and stamped one foot smartly. The rat shot away towards the wall and he saw its long pinkish tail disappear through a hole in the crumbling lath and plaster. There were dozens of holes; dozens of rats, probably. But he'd thought house rats were bigger, and *brown*. The only others he'd ever seen were fat white ones with pink eyes.

Why did he feel that he knew about rats? And why did he feel that if he got to the back of this dark little house he would find the river Thames? Memories tugged at him, then danced out of reach, floating round his bewildered head like scraps of paper caught by the wind. Warily, keeping one eye on the holes in the rotting wall, he reached the door and pulled it open gingerly.

"Thomas . . . *Thomas*! Where are you, bird?" A woman's voice, gentle even though she was shouting, and somehow familiar, came up the narrow wooden stairs.

"Leave him, mother, he's sleeping. Better to leave him." This voice was younger, different. He'd not heard it before.

"*Thomas*!" the woman called again, anxiously this time, but he took no notice. His name was Oliver, not Thomas, so she couldn't mean him. Anyway, he'd found another door at the top of the staircase. He pushed at it, and crept through.

This room was tiny and contained nothing but a bed, a small one with high sides, a bed like a coffin. There was a rough grey blanket on the floor and a small lumpy object on top of it, something with a polished round head and two stuffed legs. It looked like a doll made by a witch doctor, something evil, to stick pins in. For a minute he stayed over by the door, he'd seen movement. Rats, three or four of them, had shot away into the walls like streaks of ink. They must live in the plaster all over this house. "Runs" their escape routes were called. How *did* he know about rats? And where was his mother, fussing about getting a good set for her jam? And where were the old people?

But he didn't go looking for them, he looked through the tiny back window at the Thames; that river was more familiar to him than anything else in life. It was like breathing.

When he saw it, majestic and glittering under the hot blue sky, relief flooded over him. This was London, and he was Oliver; here was the Thames. It curved round in its old way, like an arm with its hand disappearing east, under the double railway bridge and out towards a power station. But the bridge he saw now was quite different, low-arched and narrow and cluttered with houses, and where the chimneys of the power station should have been he saw green fields, blue-edged in the haze.

The river was busy. Crude wooden dinghies, piled high with bundles, scurried under the low bridge like water beetles, heading east and out of sight. There were bigger craft too, sailing boats, their whitey-yellow canvases plump with wind. Some were moving slowly down river, others were moored to the far bank, and he could see little black figures, like stick people, going down swinging gangways with boxes and baskets, stacking things on deck. But no one was tying up and coming ashore, he noticed. They were all *leaving* London.

Oliver wiped the sweat off his face. It felt like an oven in that tiny room and his dirty brown tunic was sticking to him. Underneath he was naked. His mother always insisted on "sensible" underwear, even in summer, but he wasn't thinking about her any more; she'd become irrelevant.

He turned away from the window, crossed the room and started to creep down the stairs. Another door stood open on the floor below and through it came a sound he'd heard before, the woman's voice weeping again. Oliver stopped. He wanted to see who was there but he hated the crying, the sound of that desperate, unknown voice filled him with pain. It cut right down inside him, making him want to cry too. What was the matter with her? Why couldn't she *stop*?

He peeped round the door into a largish room, smelly and hot, and faintly smoky. There was no fire though, the smoke seemed to be coming from some little brown pots. There was one on a table, another on a shelf. They gave off a peculiar chemical smell, a bit like fireworks.

The woman sat at the table with her face in her hands and there was a girl standing behind her. They were both dressed in the same coarse brown, and their skirts swept the ground. Their long dark hair was braided and pinned up.

"Don't, mother, don't," the girl was saying, in a frightened whisper, and he saw her bend down and put her arms round the woman's neck.

"The sickness is in White's Alley, Elizabeth," he heard. "The houses are all shut up. And Biddy Skelton is taken away, and her man fled to Greenwich with the children, and 'tis come to the Marleys' house too, in Bearbinder Lane, all five of them dead, Elizabeth, and Susan, she that was my good friend . . ."

"We must pray, mother," the girl said quietly. "We must say our prayers and take comfort from the scriptures. That's what the Reverend Pearson told us to do."

"*Priests*," the weeping woman said bitterly, "and *doctors*. Where are they now when the people need them? The whole city is dying, Elizabeth, and there is no one to comfort it. Don't speak to me of Reverend Pearson. He's gone into the country, he was one of the first. It was his own skin he wanted to save."

But the girl had put a book down on the table and started to read, tracing the words with her finger like a child that barely knows its alphabet. "Unto Thee, O Lord, will I lift up my soul," she began. "My God, I have put my trust in Thee. O let me not be confounded, neither let mine enemies triumph over me. For all they that hope in Thee shall not be ashamed . . ."

The weeping gradually changed to a quiet sobbing, then stopped altogether. The woman's hands dropped from her face and she stared blankly across the smoky room. Oliver looked at her. The tear-stained face, framed in its heavy dark hair, was very beautiful. Oliver had never seen her before and yet he knew her. As the girl called Elizabeth read on, two smaller girls wandered up to the table and tried to bury themselves in the woman's skirts. He saw her arms stretch out and gather them in, like a hen gathering her chicks, and a pain shot through him. He wanted to go to her as well. In this terrifying world, a world he knew yet did not know, Oliver wanted comfort too.

At the bottom of the stairs was an oblong of dusty sunlight and a bit of cobbled street. He started padding down, on his dirty bare feet, but when he heard more voices he stopped and shrank into the shadows. The foul rotten smell was still there but now mixed with something more familiar, the clean, ordinary smell of new leather. He was looking into what appeared to be some kind of shop, the walls were lined with hooks and nails, and belts and bridles hung from them. On the floor there were crude buckets, also of leather, and a couple of saddles. A man in a greasy apron was sitting behind a long table, bending over a piece of harness.

Standing next to him was a figure that might have wandered in from a pantomime. It was immensely tall and enveloped in thick black, with huge gloves like racing gauntlets that reached almost to the elbows. Under the black robe were thick black stockings and the feet were encased in pointed black boots. It had a round, broad-brimmed hat, turned up at the edges, but the strangest part of the outfit was the hood that came right down, over the face. It reminded Oliver of a Second World War gas mask but this was black, not army green, and instead of the flat round bit that went over your nose there was a huge curved beak.

There wasn't an inch of flesh to be seen anywhere. Everything was covered with the same coarse black cloth,

and the voice that came out of the horrible beak was muffled and ghostly.

It was saying something about "the sickness", about wanting to take the bridle and go, but the saddler didn't seem to be hurrying. "There is no sickness here, Dr Craven," he told him, pulling at the bridle straps. "A man must work, and my door will stay open. If I cannot trade I cannot live. Susannah and the children are all upstairs, they are well, see for yourself. This is a clean house, believe me." But the horrible bird man was clearly anxious to leave. He kept turning his head and inspecting the dark little shop. The beak was jerking up and down and his eyeballs were gleaming through the round holes cut into the black hood.

What was he so afraid of? What was he looking for? A chill crept over Oliver as he sat hunched on the stairs and, in spite of the unnatural heat, he felt icy cold. He watched the man take his bridle in one huge, gloved hand, and he saw money fall from the other, not into the saddler's palm but into a small dish on the counter. Then, as the sinister black figure turned to go, picking up a long red stick that he held out in front of him, like a wand, his sleeve swept the dish to the floor and the contents spilled out. Oliver saw gold and silver coins rolling about, and he smelt vinegar.

He darted forward and snatched up one of the coins but before his fingers closed round it the saddler had leapt from his stool and knocked him roughly away. "Keep off, child, and go to your mother," he shouted in panic. "The sickness has come to our very door; we must touch no unclean thing. *Leave* it, Thomas!"

Oliver's cheek was stinging and he started to cry. The voice didn't sound like his at all, it was much too shrill and babyish, and it went on and on, like toddlers in supermarkets, strapped in their buggies. Then somebody picked him up and carried him back up the stairs. "Come, Thomas," she was saying, stroking his hair. "You must sleep now, and your father must work. Don't cry any more, bird."

Oliver was taken up into the tiny back room and covered up in the small box bed, the bed like a coffin. And the woman sang to him, the beautiful woman who had wept in the room below while Elizabeth read out of the Bible. "Thomas," she kept saying, "go to sleep, go to sleep, bird." And he wanted to sit up and say he was Oliver Wright, 9, Thames Terrace, London, height four feet eight inches, colour of eyes, green, phone number . . ." But his eyes began to close and the world swam away.

Everything was strange apart from the woman and he drifted off to sleep still listening to her voice. As long as she was with him it would be all right. She loved him best; he was her son.

When he opened his eyes again, night was creeping over London. He could see lights bobbing about on the dark water and more lights, scattered beyond, where the houses were. He stole through the shadowy room, reached the top of the stairs, and listened. A man was talking in the room underneath; it must be the saddler. The three box beds in the room overlooking the street were humped with bodies, all sleeping peacefully.

He crept past them, back to the window, and pressed his face against the circle he'd rubbed clean of dirt. The grizzled watchman was still standing outside the boarded-up shop. He'd lit his lantern now, and there were lights on in some of the houses too. Oliver watched him for a minute, pacing slowly up and down, then he noticed movement in the upper storey. Figures were flitting about and someone was watching the "sentry" as he walked the cobbles. Then, when the old man was at his furthest point from the house, an unseen hand pushed one of the windows open and dropped something into the street.

Oliver's eyes flew down. The thing they'd thrown out was a small soft bundle. It had hit the stones without making a sound, but it was smoking. As the watchman came back again he was looking up at the house. More windows were being opened now, and there was a loud noise of shouting and jeering from inside. They didn't want the old man to see the bundle; it was a trap.

Seconds later there was an ear-splitting explosion. Oliver's window turned white with heat and smoke, and cracked right down the middle. The sleeping bodies behind him began stirring, shook the rough blankets off and stumbled up behind him, peering out. Through a plumy haze they could see figures jumping down from the house, bundles being thrown out, snatched up by invisible fingers, and carried away. A bewildered child was handed down to a waiting woman and hustled, protesting, into the darkness. Within minutes they had emptied the house of all its occupants. There were other noises, men shouting to each other somewhere, faint, but getting nearer, and the drumming of feet. Soon their own door was unlatched and Oliver saw the top of the saddler's head, balding with a fringe of curly brown hair. He was wearing a long shirt and carrying a candlestick.

Then the screaming began. Oliver never forgot it. The girls huddled round him were screaming and the men who'd come running into the street were screaming, and his "father", the saddler, was screaming, as he stood staring down at the cobblestones, letting the candlestick clatter into the gutter. The foul smoke had almost cleared and they could see again. Oliver only looked for a second, then he turned away, choking; it was enough. The horror in the street would stay etched into his memory, as deeply and deliberately as a love-heart carved into the trunk of an old tree.

In the middle of the cobbles was a pink-red pulp, like the remains of a dog or fox mangled up by a fast car. Perched on top of it were the tatters of a pointed black hat, flapping in the small wind that blew suddenly up the narrow street from the river. The old man lay against the boarded house, staring glassily into space with eyes as round as two white marbles, but where his legs should have been there was only a dark pool, spreading slowly over the egg-shaped stones, glistening in lantern light.

The same guttering flame lit up the green studded door and its bloody cross, and on the step lay a single arm, with scraps of the plum-coloured cloak still attached to it. The hand pointed straight up at the sky and the fingers were curled round pathetically, as if begging for mercy.

Chapter Six

"Oliver? Are you all right, dear?" It was his mother's voice, anxious, and unusually kind. He opened his eyes and saw two faces, swimmy and pink at first but gradually sharpening into people he knew, Mother and Dr Verney.

He was lying on the settee in the sitting room of their flat, the old man was hovering by the door and his mother was standing over him with a damp flannel. "Are you all right?" she repeated.

"Yes, yes I think so. But what happened? I thought I was in the cellar." He sat up and rubbed at his shoulder. It felt quite sore, and he was getting a headache too. "I suppose I must have passed out," he said, in a bewildered voice.

"You suppose right," his mother added, and she sounded sharper now. "You were lying in a heap of plaster, and there's a big hole in the ceiling. It must have hit you on the head. Can you remember anything?"

"Yes, it hit me on the shoulder, actually," Oliver told her. "It was when a big trailer came past. Then I went to have another look at those cracks. I must have just passed out."

But it hadn't been like "passing out". He'd done that several times, in the dentist's, when he couldn't stand the smell. Fainting was just like falling forwards, into black cotton wool. Down in the cellar something had actually come *at* him, a force that was unseen and silent but of great strength. And he'd wanted to go with it, it was as if everything in his life had been leading up to that moment. But how could he explain a thing like that to his mother?

She was much more interested in the cracks. "I'm going to speak to the construction company tomorrow," she told him. "And the Society must be informed too. This can't go on, it'll bring the whole terrace down. Don't you agree, Dr Verney?"

The old man nodded politely, but he wasn't really listening. He had a faraway look in his eyes, and he kept staring at Oliver. Oliver stared back, his mind starting to function again as his mother dabbed at his forehead; she was at her best when people were ill. But why did Dr Verney's face seem so familiar to him, and why did he keep thinking of those people in the dream? None of them had looked a bit like the new lodger.

"Can I get up, Mum?" he said suddenly. He was perfectly all right now, and he felt hungry.

"Stay where you are for a bit, dear. I'm going to put the kettle on. Would you like a cup of tea, Dr Verney? It was kind of you to help me get Oliver upstairs." But while her back was turned the old man had slipped away, silently, like a cat.

"Funny man, isn't he?" Oliver said, getting comfortable on the settee.

"Oh, they all have their little ways," his mother shouted, above the noise of the tap filling the kettle. "He's an improvement on old Joe Porter anyhow, and he did help me get you up here. Now then, how do you feel? Do you think we should get the doctor?"

"Oh Mum, *no*. I'm perfectly all right. It's only like when I pass out at the dentist's. It stinks down in that cellar, you should get them to damp-proof it."

"But how do you *feel*, Oliver?"

"Fine. I'm fine. Can I have egg and chips for supper?" His mother didn't really approve of fatty fried food, but when he was ill he could usually get what he wanted.

"Well, all right," she said slowly, relieved to see the

colour coming back into his cheeks. "Just this once though."

While she peeled potatoes in the kitchen Oliver lay back and tried to get his mind organized. He had to face facts. It could have been a dream. Dreams were often more real and vivid than everyday life but they were nearly always muddled, with everything in the wrong order. This dream had been completely logical, with a beginning, a middle and an end. Except that he didn't want to think of the end, that legless old man, that hand.

The house in the dream was their house, or one in the same place, with the curve of the Thames at the back and the Silk Merchant's house in front. There'd been a tree under the window too, an oak tree like theirs. He had dreamed about London and Number Nine, way back in time.

In the kitchen his mother lowered the chip basket into hot fat with a satisfying sizzle. Then she began to crack eggs. It was all so familiar in the flat, so normal. His clothes were clean, he smelt of Pears Soap, and he was wearing his sensible underwear. How did he connect with that filthy, half-naked little boy, with the foul smell of the house, and with that sinister "duck man"? With the old sentry blown to pieces, as he stood in the street? Dreams were usually jumbled memories of things that had already happened to you, but Oliver's "dream" was about things he'd never seen before.

Was it a dream?

It was like a very complicated jigsaw puzzle and so far he'd only got a handful of pieces, the family and the house, and the river, with its queer little boats. Ted Hoskins was part of it too though, Ted and his "darkness". He was sure about that. And so was Dr Verney.

One thing fitted already, that cross the yobbos had painted on their front door. He'd seen a red cross in his dream.

A few days later, after school, he knocked on the door of Dr Verney's bedsitter. His father hadn't been much help over his "stone". He'd not been able to decipher the marks, not even with his reading glasses. He'd been doubtful they meant anything anyway. "But this Dr Verney might help," he'd told Oliver. "He may well have a good magnifying glass, and he sounds quite an interesting old chap. Show it to him."

"I *will*," Oliver said. He was pleased. His mother had stopped fretting over Dad so much because he was recovering well from his operation. In fact, she was altogether more good-tempered these days.

He did want to borrow a magnifying glass but he also wanted to see inside Dr Verney's room. The old man was very secretive. He always hurried past if you met him in the street, and whenever they passed on the stairs he shot up to his bedsitter like a frightened rabbit. There was definitely something odd about him.

He wasn't going to let Oliver in at first, but the minute he saw the little black stone he seemed to change his mind. His whole body went stiff when he took it in his hand, and a pale pink flush crept slowly over his shrivelled face. "Come in, Oliver," he said, his wavery old man's voice quite shrill with excitement, "I'm no historian, you understand, but I can certainly tell you a little about this. May I ask how you came by it?"

While Oliver was explaining about Geoff and the building site his eyes were wandering round the room. It was bare and comfortless with nothing to show it belonged to anyone, except a load of books and papers. It was like a room in a hospital, or an hotel.

Some things were odd though. The bed had been stripped, for one thing, right down to the mattress, and the sheets, red and brown with a jazzy modern pattern, were draped over the radiator. "Those aren't ours," said

Oliver. He was very familiar with the Society's plain white bed linen. One of his jobs was to tie it all up on Tuesday afternoons, ready for the laundry man. Fancy an old man like this having such trendy sheets.

"No, that's quite right. I bought them in John Lewis's. Nice, aren't they?" Dr Verney said gleefully. When he smiled he looked like a little boy. Oliver stared at him, faintly uneasy. Why did he keep thinking he knew him? "Didn't you like Mum's sheets then?" he blurted out.

"Oh yes, very nice, best quality Egyptian cotton, I noticed. But they're *white* you see, Oliver, and I can't have white. They go for it."

He'd turned his back and was studying the stone with a large magnifying glass. Oliver repeated what he'd said to himself. "*White* . . . they *go* for it . . ." Who on earth were "they"? Housebreakers, out to steal a couple of sheets from an old man? Dr Verney was round the bend.

As he studied the room more carefully he became more and more convinced of it. Every last crack in the door and the skirting boards had been stuffed with paper. "Mice, you see, Oliver, rats and mice," he was informed. "It won't stop them if they're really determined, but it's the best I can do till I can think of something more permanent."

It was getting odder by the minute. What was that little copper bowl on the window sill, smoking gently and giving off a sickly, sweet smell? He pointed to it. "Is that a joss stick, Dr Verney?"

The old man glanced at it, looked down at Oliver, and hesitated. "Well, no, not exactly. It's a – I suppose you could describe it as a kind of air-freshener, something I put together myself. I'm a bit of an inventor really."

Oliver was thoughtful. If he wanted to freshen up his room why didn't he just open the window? And why couldn't he buy some Air-Wick, or one of those sprays from Sainsbury's? His mother would have something to say about this room, if she ever managed to get inside, what with new jazzy sheets, and home-made "air fresheners". That smoking bowl could start a fire.

"There you are, Oliver," Dr Verney was saying, "Look at that. It's extremely worn, and you'll have to hold the glass steady. But there's no doubt at all as to what it is. What a find!"

Oliver took his stone and looked through the glass. He saw five letters arranged in a pattern –

ABRACADABRA
ABRACADABR
ABRACADAB
ABRACADA
ABRACAD
ABRACA
ABRAC
ABRA
ABR
AB
A

"Abra . . . cad . . . abra . . ." he muttered slowly, "Abracadabra . . . Is it a sort of charm?

"Right first time!" Dr Verney patted him on the head, and held his hand out. "It is worn to keep away evil, Oliver. Round the neck probably, hence the hole."

"What kind of evil?" Oliver didn't much like the way the old man was trying to take his stone. Ted Hoskins' "attack" on the building site had been about evil, so had the blackness that had surged through their cellar, swallowing him up. Dr Verney might be "evil" too.

"Oh, illness, gossip, that sort of thing," the old man said vaguely. "Of course, there's no saying how old it is. It will take me some time to establish that. If you would just leave it with me . . ."

"No," Oliver said firmly, and he put the stone in his pocket. "I want my dad to have a look at it first. He gets bored in the hospital and a thing like this will interest him." Dr Verney wasn't to know that his father had already seen the stone but it was vital to hold on to it. If the old man took it away Oliver had a strong suspicion that he'd never see it again.

"Well, of course, Oliver, I do understand." But his voice was different, angry almost, and his small glittery eyes were looking covetously at the boy's trouser pocket. "I would very much like to look after it for a while, that's all, then perhaps I can work out its history. Do you see?"

Oliver made polite excuses about "helping his mother", and left. He'd got a hunch about this odd-looking stone, and he'd no intention of handing it over to Dr Verney. In fact, when he fell asleep that night, it was in the safest possible place, on a string round his neck.

Chapter Seven

Next morning Tracey Bell pounced on him the minute he walked through the school gates. "He's got one," she whispered triumphantly, "and he says we can have it. I'm bringing it to school with me on Monday."

Oliver backed away. He didn't want people looking at them, and Tracey's idea of a whisper was like other people shouting their heads off. "What are you talking about?" he said, "What's 'it'?"

"Rats. He's got a couple of rats in his shop, and he's letting us have the baby one for that telly programme. Good, i'n't? He's sending us a book as well, so you'll know what to feed it on and that."

Oliver didn't like the "you". Why was she pushing it all on to him? "I'm . . . I'm not sure," he said vaguely, trying to get away.

"But Oll, we *agreed*. You said it could go down your cellar, you said you'd ask your mum and everything. *Have* you asked her?"

"Well, no," he admitted, in an embarrassed grunt. Tracey had gone very red in the face. She looked as if she might cry.

"But you promised. I'd get it from Uncle Len and you'd . . . you *promised*, Oliver."

"I know, I know," he said feebly, "Look, keep your voice down, can't you? Everyone's looking at us. You don't want people copying our idea. I mean," he added slyly, "I don't suppose anyone else'll be getting a rat."

That did it. Tracey subsided against the school wall like a popped balloon, and waited for him to go on. She really admired Oliver. If he'd only do the telly project with her they'd be bound to get picked. He was dead clever.

When he looked at that hopeful pink face he felt mean. She was obviously dying to appear with Kit McKenzie, showing off her Uncle Len's rat, and if he backed out she wouldn't have a chance. He shouldn't have agreed in the first place. "Well, I'll have another look in the cellar," he said slowly, playing for time. "It's just that Mum's got a lot on her mind at the moment, with my dad in hospital and everything, and she's not too keen on me having a pet," (and that was putting it mildly). "Don't tell *your* mum, for heaven's sake," he added sharply.

"Why not?"

"Because she might mention it to mine when she starts the job. You'll just have to keep quiet about it, Tracey."

"But what about getting it from Uncle Len?"

"That's your problem," he said heartlessly, secretly hoping she might scrap the whole idea. But something in those determined little eyes of hers told him that she wouldn't.

After school he called in at River Reach to see if there was any useful rubbish going. If he'd got to have this rat he was going to do the job properly, and he could make it a run. It'd be cruel to keep it cooped up in a little cage all the time and the floor of the cellar was massive stone slabs so it couldn't burrow into that. Oliver was quite good with his hands. He was sure he could rig something up if he could find some fine wire mesh. All kinds of stuff got thrown into those huge skips at the building site. It saved people going to the dump.

On the way he passed St Olave's churchyard with its peculiar raised oval of grass. It was almost level with his waist, and he wasn't exactly tall. He'd always thought it was odd, standing up above the street like that.

Oliver clambered up on to the grass and spotted the spindly black figure of Dr Verney bent over a cockeyed tombstone. Well, *that* wasn't going to tell him anything. The letters had been worn away years ago. They'd moved most of the headstones, anyway, when they pulled the church down. What was left had been neatly arranged round the oval of grass, like a fence. His mother had tried to stop them doing that; she thought it showed disrespect to the dead.

The old man straightened up slowly, rubbed his back with one stiff, knobbled hand, then peered thoughtfully all round, first at the graveyard, then along Thames Terrace to Number Nine, then back towards the demolition site at River Reach. He'd cupped his chin in his hand and he was frowning. It was obvious that he was trying to work something out. What, though?

Oliver left him to it and headed for the building site. It was quite late and they were already packing up to go home. There was still no sign of Ted Hoskins, and no sign of sour-faced Rick either. Geoff was there though, pulling his jacket on and checking the locks on a shed that had been put up to store some of the smaller tools in. Oliver's eyes gleamed when he saw a large yellow skip piled high with promising-looking rubbish. There'd been no skips for ages.

"Can I have this, Geoff?" he shouted, fishing out a piece of crumpled chicken wire. If he flattened it out it might make a run for the rat.

"Well, I suppose so," the man muttered, doing up his zipper. "What on earth do you want it for?"

"Oh, you know . . ." Oliver said mysteriously, peering into the depths of the skip. "Anything interesting turned up lately?"

"Ne'er, not really, not what you'd call interesting. No bodies, if that's what you're getting at," and the man grinned. He thought Oliver was hilarious, with his interest in blood and gore, and those horror comics he was always reading.

"Nothing at all? What do you mean, 'not really'?"

"Well, I found these. I kept them out for you, but when you didn't turn up I chucked them back, with all the other rubbish. Hang on." He bent over the side of the skip and rooted about, then he flung something over his shoulder, a dark, dampish object that hit Oliver in the chest.

"Hang on, here's the other. Perhaps they'll make you a pair. *Catch*!"

Oliver stared at the things in his hands. At first he could make nothing of them, they were just curling, cardboardy lumps. Then he looked more closely, moving his fingers over them. He could see stitching now, and lines of tiny pinpoints where a needle had gone in and out. They were tiny shoes, and, in spite of all those years in the cloggy London soil, he could still detect a faint leathery smell, a smell that took him back to the terrifying duck man, and to his "dream".

"Geoff! Come here, will you! What the hell are you doing leaving this out?" It was Rick the foreman, standing over by the site entrance, holding up a pick. Oliver fled. The man had already told him off twice for going through the skips. If he saw him with this stuff he'd have it off him, just for spite. Rick was like that. And Oliver wanted to hold on to the sodden little shoes. Very dimly and gradually, like a film slowed right down, a pattern had started to form.

These shoes were part of it. Shoes meant feet, and feet meant people. Grown-ups often lied to children and, whatever Geoff had told him about there being no mystery at River Reach, Oliver knew that everything had started there. He wanted to take the shoes home, up to his attic room, to think about them. Ted Hoskins was part of the pattern, and so was Dr Verney. Oliver was more and more certain about it now.

When he saw Rick striding towards the skip he shoved

the chicken wire under his arm, and squeezed through a gap in the fence, still clutching his shoes. Then he tore down Thames Terrace with a thumping heart. The sodden leather was making a damp patch on his sweater and, under his shirt, the abracadabra stone bobbed up and down.

As he let himself into Number Nine he saw an unfamiliar car parked outside. In the hall he heard voices floating up from the cellar; it was an official from the Council, talking to his mother about the cracks.

Oliver hid his treasures in the cubbyhole under the stairs and crept down the steps. They were standing by the grating, staring at the front wall. "I can see what you mean, Mrs Wright," the dark-suited man was saying, "but I think you have a difficulty. You see, there's no way of proving that this damage is directly related to the increased load of traffic. I'm sure that's the line they'll take."

"Rubbish!" said his mother. "It's perfectly obvious what's brought this about. The whole terrace shakes when they come down here with all that heavy equipment. You ask the people next door."

"Yes, but as I say, responsibility is difficult to *prove*. How long is it, for example, since you yourself came down here? This wall may have been deteriorating for some considerable time, without you really noticing."

There was an abrupt silence. The man was absolutely right. It was months since his mother had been in the cellar. She always sent him down for things. Oliver began making his way towards them but there was something slightly odd about the way the two figures were standing by the flaking white wall, black figures with no faces, two backs, mumbling at one another. And he didn't want to go near those cracks at all. It was happening again, just like the first time. He was being pulled silently forwards, almost as if there were little wheels on his feet.

Someone had started to cry, the woman's voice again, the

low, desperate moaning that went on and on, relentlessly. At first it sounded as if it was coming from the street, then out of the damp walls, then, somehow, out of his own brain. It was a very small sound at first, but curiously intense, strengthening minute by minute till it was strident, insistent, making the other two voices a meaningless burble.

"STOP IT!" he shouted suddenly, shaking his head from side to side. Something in the voice made him want to scream back, the pain and anguish in it was somehow his pain.

"Oliver!" His mother whipped round, and stared at him. He stared too, but not at her, and not at the bald, bespectacled official who was peering at him owlishly in the gloom. The cracks were widening and growing longer, and the dark coming out of them was suffocating and thick, swirling round his head like a dense fog. He looked desperately for a face in the darkness, someone to comfort. Anything to stop that terrible screaming noise.

"What on earth's the matter, Oliver?" his mother was saying snappily. "What are you staring at?"

"I feel a bit sick," he mumbled. "I think I'll have to go back upstairs, and get some fresh air . . ." But even as the words came from his lips he was falling, falling forwards into that awful blackness and it came and took him, dropping down over him like a cloak.

Chapter Eight

"I don't *want* to go there, I want to see the boats!" It was Oliver's own voice, but tearful and a bit squeaky, and he was being dragged along a narrow street, away from the river.

"We must buy meat, Thomas," a girl's voice was saying wearily. "Mother says there's a butcher still trading, in Bearbinder Lane. Bread too, if we can find it."

"Mother makes our bread," he was saying sulkily, kicking at her ankles through the coarse brown skirt. "I want to see the boats, I don't *want* bread." And he sat down howling on the cobbles.

"Come, Thomas," she said, cuddling him. "Abigail's sick, she has a fever. Mother can't make the bread today." But he went on grizzling, with his sister's arms round him, watching a sleek black rat creep along the gutter.

"I want to see the *boats*," he whined, as she tried to get him back on his feet.

"All right. I will take you to the river. But then we must find Bearbinder Lane. Mother said we mustn't be away too long from the house."

"Why does Abigail have the fever?" he said, but he didn't listen to the answer. He'd got what he wanted now and he was trotting along quite cheerfully, holding her hand. They were leaving the huddle of gables and smoking chimneys behind and he could see green fields. But there was no sweet country smell. Everything reeked of rot and decay. Human dung was piled outside some of the doors, with rats running over it, and at the side of a tiny barn-like church he saw a huge mound. It was an odd knobbly shape and it was covered with a sprinkling of freshly-dug soil. The mound looked sinister in the warm sunshine and the smell coming out of it was so terrible that Oliver started heaving; his tiny stomach felt as if it was being pummelled like a punch-bag.

"Come away, Tom," the girl said, in a frightened whisper. "Don't go near that. Here, hold this to your face." A soft rag was pushed into his hand and he covered his nose with it. It smelt of herbs, sickly-sweet, and he didn't like it much, but anything was better than the smell coming out of that peculiar mound.

As they hurried along he glanced up at his sister. She was white-faced and anxious, and she was holding his hand far too tight, as if she thought someone might come leaping out at them, and spirit him away. There was something round her neck on a chain, an animal of some sort, a frog, all made out of silver. His fingers crept up to his own neck. He was wearing a chain too, with a queer little stone on. When his mother taught him to read he'd be able to read what it said. She was already teaching Abigail and even Sarah, his youngest sister, knew her alphabet. The words on the stone were magic, like the frog. They had to wear them all the time, to keep the sickness away.

"I can see the river!" he shouted jubilantly. There it was, a precious snatch of blue at the end of a long alley. "Come *on*, Elizabeth." He tugged at her hand, but she was hesitating. "We ought to go home, Thomas," she said nervously. "I have only been out as far as this with Father."

"Are we lost?" He was desperate to see the great river with all its boats, the people leaving the city with their bags and bundles. But the look in her pinched white face had put fear into him, she was so scared-looking. It was that mound.

He still pulled her along the alley towards the river, tugging at her skirt like a puppy, but all the time her eyes were flicking from side to side at the silent, sealed-up houses, each with a crude red cross daubed on the door, and sometimes the words "Lord, Have Mercy!" He'd seen lots of those crosses, there were some in their street too. It was because of the sickness.

At the end of the alley there was a small landing place where steps went down to the water, but they couldn't get through. A tall cloaked figure with a pike and a cone-shaped hat stood blocking the way. When it heard their shoes on the cobblestones it turned round and shoved its pike at them. "Get away from here, get home!" it shouted. "Nobody can pass through here." It was a bent old man, his crumpled face wreathed in dirty grey whiskers. Oliver clutched at his sister's arm. A man like this had been blown to pieces in their own street; he'd been on guard duty too. But why couldn't they go down to the river?

"I want to see the boats," he whimpered hopefully. Grizzles and whines worked, especially with old people. But his answer was a stinking, tangled beard thrust into his face, and the curved blade of the pike inches from his button nose. "Come away, Thomas," Elizabeth whispered, pulling him away from the steps. "We must go to Bearbinder Lane."

But as they went back up the street, dung sticking to the soles of their little shoes, and the rags held up to their faces, to stop the smell choking them, there was a sudden terrible screaming noise.

Elizabeth stopped and pulled him back into a doorway. Whoever was screaming had turned the corner and was running along the alley. As people tore past Oliver peeped out from the folds of her skirt and saw him.

It was a man, stark naked, his whole body covered with

great coloured blotches. The reds and browns of the huge patches were so violent they might have been put on with paint. There were frayed cords flapping from his wrists and ankles, as if he'd been tied up but had somehow broken free. "Let me get to the water, for Christ in Heaven's name," he was screaming. "Let me see the *water*!" And his voice was agony in Oliver's ears, the tearing cries of pain were like nothing he had ever heard. It was as if they were being ripped out of living flesh.

As the man got to the steps the pike blade came up and the old guard cut at him, but the man was too strong. He grabbed the wooden pole and broke it across his knees like a piece of firewood, then he pushed the terrified man into the gutter, slavering and howling at him like a mad dog. Then he jumped into the river.

Somebody was pulling the petrified watchman to his feet again; there was a great gash down one cheek, where the pike blade had sliced it, and blood was pouring out. The other men stood huddled together, staring out helplessly across the Thames, the far bank nothing more than a blur in the blistering heat. No one had noticed the two children and Oliver crept between a forest of legs, looking for the mad man.

"Poor soul," a voice muttered. They could see his arms threshing about in the water, the hideously bruised back, humping up and down, as he struck out for the opposite shore. But the river was much wider here than Oliver had ever seen it, and he watched the man slow down, and go under, his head disappearing at last in a flurry of little bubbles.

The last agonized scream that echoed across the water as it closed over him rang in Oliver's brain for months afterwards, the scream, and the sight of one desperate white hand, stretching straight up out of the river towards the flat blue sky.

"He's gone," whispered Elizabeth, crossing herself and shepherding him away, along the alley. "Come, Thomas, we must go back. We've been out too long already."

"But why was he running away?" he asked her. "Why was he screaming? And why did he have those marks all over him?"

"It was the sickness, lamb. He had the tokens."

"But why was he *screaming*?"

"Because . . . because he was in pain. When the tokens are on you the doctors can do nothing. He knew that. His life was over."

"Well, I think he was running away from *them*," the little boy said stoutly, puffing a bit because Elizabeth was walking too fast. "I think they were trying to kill him."

"No, Tom," she said quietly. "His agonies drove him to it. We should pray for him."

"Abigail doesn't have the sickness, does she, Elizabeth?" and he looked up into her face, suddenly anxious.

"Goodness no, just a little fever. Mother said so. Look, we're back in Crown Street and that leads straight into Bearbinder Lane." But her voice had a dead feel to it, and she would not look at him.

The man in Bearbinder Lane gave them meat wrapped in a bit of sacking and pushed a little bowl of vinegar across his counter. She dropped three coins in it, grasped Oliver's hand, and turned quickly away. The city was deathly quiet. There were no bread sellers out on the streets, no market women with milk and eggs, only a crone holding out a wooden tray on a corner. "What do ye lack, ladies?" she croaked, as they hurried past. "What do ye lack?" The tray had fish on it, stinking to high heaven and crawling with flies.

It was ghostly in the narrow streets. The cobbled alleys and the market squares were empty and echoing, grass greening the stones. Door after door carried its glaring cross and Oliver ran down one long passage-way letting the marks flash by him, like soldiers marching. They only saw two passers-by between Bearbinder Lane and their own street, and both crossed over to the other side, to avoid contact, muffling their faces in cloaks and shawls in spite of the heat. "What are they doing that for?" Oliver wanted to know. "They can't see if they do that. They might fall over."

"The sickness is in the air, Tom. You must not breathe it."

"But we've not got it, have we? I've got my charm."

"No, we've not got the sickness, God be praised."

At the end of their street people had made fires outside their houses and men stood poking at the smoking heaps with sticks. "It's to cleanse the air, Tom," his sister told him, before he could open his mouth, "like Mother's doing at home, with her dish of sweet herbs."

He liked bonfires; he wanted to stop and help them get a really good blaze, but Elizabeth was pulling him along. Why did the smell of the smoke and that little dish in the low, dark saddler's house seem so familiar to him? What were these shadowy memories, tugging at his brain? He was in Tom's body, Thomas, the saddler's youngest child, and that sweet-faced woman waiting at home was his mother. But he was Oliver too, Oliver Wright of 9, Thames Terrace.

Yet he could not tell them. The world he was locked in had stopped his mouth with the weight of its unfolded centuries. He was only a five year old urchin, who didn't even know his alphabet.

The woman was looking out for them and as soon as they stepped into the house she snatched him up and pushed Elizabeth before her, up the stairs. A violent argument seemed to be going on in the saddler's shop. As he was carried away Oliver twisted his head round and looked back at the huge hooked shadow on the wall. It was the duck man.

"She will *recover*," his father was shouting desperately. "My wife Susannah is a good nurse, she watches her day and night. She is sure the fever is abating. If you shut us away in this house I cannot trade, Dr Craven, and if I cannot trade I cannot live. What will become of us, in God's name? I have six mouths to feed."

"You must stay here till the house is clean again," the duck man told him, his muffled voice mechanical and toneless, as if he had said all this a thousand times before. "Food will be brought to you, and water. They will be left outside by the door. You are not alone in your troubles, John. The whole city groans in its agony. The house must be sealed. The order has gone out already. May God have mercy on you, and save you."

As his mother shut the upper door Oliver heard a great roar of anger from his father. "Hypocrite! If you lock us up in this house you condemn us to death, like all the others. Abigail has a mild fever, a child's complaint. If you shut us away – "

"She has the *marks* upon her, John, the old woman said so."

Then the street door slammed shut, and there was silence.

It was dark in the room, and Oliver's eyes ached, trying to focus. None of the glaring summer brightness spilled into the airless shadows, the windows were too small. As he got used to the dim light he saw the blurred figures more plainly. His middle sister, Abigail, lay on a straw mattress under a coarse grey sheet. Her eyes were closed but she tossed and moaned continuously, and her mother knelt on the floor beside her with a basin of water, wiping her face and hands with a rag, and whispering to her. But the soft voice only seemed to madden her, making her arms and legs thrash about more wildly. The sheet slid off and Oliver saw to his horror that she was tied to the mattress with cords, pulled tight and making red weals across her chest and thighs. There were faint, bluish patches too, round marks coming up on her face and neck, like bruises.

His little sister Sarah was whimpering and burrowing into his mother's skirts. Elizabeth stood by the fireplace, hollow-eyed and staring, and there was someone with her, a tiny bent figure shrunk into a chair, an old woman in grey-brown rags.

Oliver stared at the shrivelled face and it struck terror into him. There was something pitiless about the small, hard eyes, the pinched mouth, and she was looking curiously at the figure on the bed, looking at the small silver charm round her neck. His fingers felt under his tunic for his own little stone, and clutched it tight.

The sick child gave a sudden, deafening scream and struggled to get up, and Oliver saw beads of blood where the cords had cut into her. "She is tied too tightly," his mother said to the old woman. "We should loosen the bindings."

"*No*," and she was by the straw pallet in a flash. "She must stay bound, till the sickness passes."

"But when will it pass?" His mother's voice was scarcely a whisper and she put her arm round Sarah who was whining and backing away from the sinister bent figure in its filthy rags.

"In God's good time," the old woman said piously, crossing herself with knotted fingers. But Oliver didn't believe her. He saw only death in that narrow, grasping face.

Elizabeth put him to bed in his little box, in the stuffy back room overlooking the river. It felt too early for sleep and it was still light outside, but the door was shut on him, and he was left there.

He lay awake for a long time, itchy and hot under his blanket, listening to noises. Far away, seagulls mewed over the Thames; nearer, he could hear a blur of voices in the room below, and the odd piercing cry from his sister Abigail. Behind his head rats scrabbled and scratched in the walls.

Doors slammed shut in the street, and a man shouted; then there was silence. But somewhere in the city a solitary bell was ringing and, as sleep crept over him at last, he could hear it getting nearer. It was a hand bell, rung in stops and starts, and he could hear the clopping of a horse too. Whatever it was was nearing the house.

Then the sounds were drowned by a terrific banging. Someone down below was hammering on their front door, but nobody went to open it. The noise went on and on until the murmur of voices down below suddenly broke off. All he could hear now were the shrieks of his sister Abigail, shrieks almost as loud and terrible as the man who had thrown himself in the river. And under the shrill child's voice there was an awful undertow, a noise that was as familiar to him now as his own small body. It was the helpless weeping of his mother as she sat watching over her dying child.

Carefully, he unlatched his own door and crept through. The front bedroom was empty but he'd only taken one step inside when he shrank back again. A man was at the window, on a ladder. He'd got nails in his mouth and he was hammering big flat pieces of wood across the windows; Oliver could hear him whistling. The two planks made the shape of a cross. There would be a cross on the door too, Christ's cross, dripping red, daubed from a leather bucket like the ones his father sold in the shop. His sister Abigail had got the sickness, and their house was being sealed up because it was unclean.

When the man had gone he went back to his own room. The day was ebbing away now and the planks made a huge black X, dark upon light. But there was still enough window left for him to see out, and he stretched up, pressing his face to the glass.

Someone was walking up and down outside the house. He could just see a cone-shaped hat and the top of a pike. Backwards and forwards. Stop. Backwards and forwards. Then he heard the tinny bell being rung again, the clopping horse, and the rattle of wheels on cobbles, and an open cart came down past the house, with two men walking alongside. They were laughing loudly and one was sucking on a long clay pipe. He kept turning round to inspect his load, and blowing smoke over it.

The other belched, wiped his mouth, and rooted about in the cart with a hooked pole. "Faggots for sale!" he roared up at the silent houses. "Good young faggots for sale!" Some of the pieces were sticking straight up in the air; they looked rather funny.

The man with the pipe took a pole and ambled away, out of sight, ringing his bell; the other stayed holding the horse's head. Only when he pulled on the leathers and moved the cart forward, dislodging the load, did Oliver realize that they weren't selling sticks at all because something was lolling down, over the high wooden sides. It was a head, a woman's head with a sweep of long, dark hair that got caught up in the painted spokes as the wheels crunched forwards. The faggots piled up for burning were human legs.

Chapter Nine

This time Oliver got himself up to the flat with his mother close behind him, supplying a running commentary. He'd only been "out" for a couple of minutes, and she'd been more embarrassed than worried. "Screaming like that," she told him, "when the man from the Council was there. I can't imagine what he must have thought. You've got to stop all this *reading*, Oliver, it's not doing you any good. Heaven knows what you'd be like if we had a television with all the rubbish they put on."

"Dad likes me reading," he said meekly, flopping down on the settee. "Anyway, I'd not had any dinner at school, that's probably why it happened."

"And whose fault's that? How many times have I told you to eat up . . . ?"

"It was revolting, Mum."

"Now don't exaggerate."

"It *was*. One giant fish finger and some sloppy baked beans. Why can't I take sandwiches? Everyone else does."

"Because a growing child needs a hot meal in the middle of the day. And you've not been wearing your vest again, have you? You've obviously got a chill on your stomach. You're not strong, Oliver . . ."

"Mum, it's *June*! Nobody wears vests in *June*! When I get changed for P.E. they all laugh."

"Let them," she said fiercely. "Why be like everyone else? I'll tell you this, though. If we have any more of these fainting fits I'm taking you to see the doctor."

Oliver said nothing. It was easier to let her go on. It wasn't a "faint", anyway. It was like the first time. The men at River Reach had disturbed something while they were digging, then that cross had appeared on their door, then Dr Verney had shown up. Their own house was at the centre of it, he knew that now.

The actual house over the ancient cellar had been altered and enlarged several times, ripped down twice at least, and built all over again. But the ancient foundations had never been touched. History had printed itself on the mouldy, knobbled walls, the stones themselves had absorbed the pain and suffering of centuries, like a tape recorder that went on for ever. Now something was making it play everything back.

His mother was still nagging at him. "I've got enough to worry about, Oliver, with your father still in hospital, and getting Mrs Bell into the cleaning routine – and Dr Verney's a worry too. I really don't think I should have accepted him."

"*Mum*," he said very loudly, in a voice that meant "Shut up!" and he pointed at the sitting room door. It had opened suddenly, and the old man was standing there, staring at them.

Mrs Wright bristled. It was absolutely against the rules to have residents wandering into their private flat. If they needed anything urgently they had bells in their rooms, bells that rang in her kitchen. He must have opened their front door, and let himself in. It was bare-faced cheek.

"Sorry to bother you, Mrs Wright," he said politely, looking round the flat, "but I wondered if you'd be good enough to come down and look at my bed?"

"Your *bed*?" Her mouth dropped open, and she raised her eyebrows at Oliver, but he was dying to laugh, and he looked away.

"Well, I just wondered if there were mice in it. I don't sleep very well, you see, there's so much noise."

"Noise? What sort of noise? You're right at the back of

the house and anyway this street's very quiet at night. As for *mice* in your room, well really, Dr Verney . . ."

"But it's so near the river, Mrs Wright, therefore it's quite possible that voles and mice get into the house from time to time, rats even. I can definitely hear scratching noises in the walls, and it worries me. I'm sure the health authority ought to know."

"*Rats*?" she repeated. "I'm sorry, Dr Verney, but you must be out of your mind."

Oliver winced. His mother wasn't strong on tact, not even with the old people, and she was getting really angry now. She'd be telling the old man to pack his bags in a minute, he knew the signs. "If you're not satisfied you can go, whenever you want," she said. "In fact, it might be better all round if you did. There's no need to stay for the month, I can refund your rent. Just let me find the Society's cheque book . . ."

"Oh no, no, *no*, Mrs Wright. I'm very satisfied, I *must* stay here."

"Must? I'm afraid I don't understand. The Society has other houses, modern places, purpose-built. You wouldn't worry so much if you were in one of those."

"This is where I must be," the old man said simply. "And if you could just look at my bed I'd rest easier then."

"I'll come and have a look," Oliver said, jumping up. "I don't mind mice." It was a crafty move because it meant his mother would have to come too; it was one way for him to get a look inside the old man's room. She scowled at him but Dr Verney was already going down the stairs. "Perhaps I could borrow Mrs MacDougall's cat for a few days," he said, over his shoulder. "That would get rid of them."

"There's nothing to get rid *of*, Dr Verney," Oliver's mother called out, in a voice that was bursting with suppressed rage. But Oliver was already halfway down the stairs and she had to follow on. She'd have words with him later though, when they'd sorted this potty old man out.

It didn't take very long because she swept through the room like a whirlwind, poking and prying, and asking dozens of questions. The bed was stripped in two minutes flat, right down to the mattress, and the jazzy sheets and pillowcases shaken out, under his nose. "*There*, do you see, Dr Verney? Nothing to worry about at all, is there? Now if you don't mind we'll have the other sheets back on, it's much easier when I do the laundry," and she proceeded to remake the bed, helped by Oliver.

He was feeling a bit sorry for the old man now. He'd looked positively crushed as the housekeeper stormed about his little room. "But they *go* for white," he protested feebly. "It's a scientific fact." She ignored him and carried on plumping up the pillows, though she shot a look at Oliver, a look that said, beyond all possible doubt, that she thought Dr Thomas Verney was slowly going off his head.

He protested rather more vigorously when she removed the smoking bowl from his windowsill. "I have it to cleanse the air," he explained, as she carried it through the door, at arm's length. "It's most effective, you see. I made it myself, to a special recipe."

"Well, I've got some proper air fresheners in my kitchen cupboard," she told him. "Oliver can bring one up later. We can't have this, Dr Verney. It's a fire hazard. Do you want the whole house to go up in smoke? Now, if you don't mind, I must make our evening meal or I'll be late for the hospital," and she swept out with Oliver, leaving the old man staring after them, clasping and unclasping his hands.

"He'll have to go," she said firmly, as they sat at the supper table. "I'm taking a writing pad into the hospital with me, your father can help me put a letter together, to send to the Society. I've already complained to them but they're not being at all helpful. His file's gone missing or something. I've tried ringing that daughter of his myself. Couldn't get through. The operator told me it was a 'discontinued number'; she must have moved, I suppose."

Oliver ate his poached egg on toast without comment, and stirred his tea thoughtfully. "I must live here", that's what the old man had said. *Must*? Something had attracted Dr Verney to their house, and something was keeping him here; something much stronger than his neurotic fear of the rats and mice, nibbling at his toes as he lay in bed; something stronger than the "things" that liked white sheets. He was both attracted and repelled by Number Nine, Thames Terrace – it was like Oliver and death. It terrified him, yet he couldn't leave it alone.

And now the old man's official file had disappeared, and nobody answered the phone at the daughter's house. That was odd, too. Oliver chewed a bun and started to daydream. Perhaps, when Dr Verney went into his bedsitter and shut the door, he actually disappeared. Oliver had decided he was a ghost, the very first time he saw him.

The front door slammed down below, and he got up and looked through the window. The "ghost" was striding purposefully down the street, with some books under his arm. "He must be going to the library," Oliver told his mother. "It's their late night. He'll have to get a move on, it shuts in half an hour."

"He's never *away* from the library," she muttered disapprovingly, as though books were dangerous. "He sits there for hours, reading through the back numbers of the local paper. Mrs MacDougall told me."

"Well, he's interested in history. Nothing wrong with that, is there?" Oliver said daringly. Once his mother got her knife into someone she really twisted it, and he didn't want her to drive Dr Verney out of the house. He didn't understand what was happening but he'd got one of his hunches; this old man had simply got to stay.

"I don't want you to come to the hospital tonight," his mother informed him, pulling her coat on. "You're looking a bit washed-out and I don't want you worrying your father. Answer the phone, if it rings, and tell them I'll be back at half past eight."

Oliver tried to look sorrowful and disappointed about missing the hospital visit, but he was secretly delighted. It meant he could make a proper inspection of Dr Verney's bedsitter. The minute his mother shut the front door he removed her "master key" from the kitchen, hopped down the stairs and let himself in.

The old man had remade his bed with the jazzy sheets and the white ones lay neatly folded on a chair. There was another little bowl smoking away on the windowsill. Oliver took it over to the wash basin and ran cold water on it. His mother was right about the fire hazard; if a house like Number Nine went up in flames it would be difficult getting everyone out. He couldn't see Mrs MacDougall jumping into a fireman's blanket with Binkie.

He looked round and counted seven different canisters of fly spray. "Deadly to all common pests" he read on one. "Kills Every Known Household Insect" said another. And the room smelt awful, chemical fumes from the bowl mixed with fly spray and "Woodland Fern" from his mother's air freshener. He opened the window and flapped his hands about. The old man would think it was his mother, after today's goings on.

In one corner there was a rickety old card table which Dr Verney was obviously using as a desk. There were several books on it, and some neat stacks of paper covered with fine black handwriting. Oliver glanced at the top sheet but it was impossible to read without a magnifying glass. There were more books under the table, and more in toppling heaps by the bed. The pale green walls were quite bare except for a very large map of London, and someone had been drawing big circles on it with black ink. They were all over the place, like black balloons. A bit of Thames Terrace was in one, together with St Olave-le-Strand, the old church they'd pulled down last year.

The thing that interested him most was an old box on a shelf over the bed. It was studded with nails and bound with brass hoops, and it had a curved lid, like a miniature pirate's chest. Oliver's fingers itched to take it down, a box like that was just asking to be opened. But as he stretched up for it he heard someone opening the front door.

It couldn't be Dr Verney, he'd have only just reached the library, but it might be his mother, coming back for something she'd forgotten, and if she found him in the old man's room there'd be big trouble. He didn't want to go yet, he'd only just started his investigations, but he was frightened of her when she got in a real temper, and it was important not to annoy her, because of the rat.

As he turned away from Dr Verney's "desk" he noticed a scrap of paper weighted down with a bottle of ink. He picked it up and tried to decipher the spidery handwriting. It looked like odd notes, jotted down from reference books. "*White* – " he read, "curiously, the flea is very attracted to white objects and it is found for preference on white fabrics, bedclothes or clothing." Underneath, in shaky block capitals, it said, "THE BACILLUS CAN SURVIVE FOR MONTHS AND SOMETIMES EVEN FOR YEARS IF KEPT IN THE DARK, PARTICULARLY IN THE MICROCLIMATE OF RODENTS' BURROWS . . ."

*

"I've forgotten your father's clean pyjamas," his mother told him, foraging about in a drawer. He'd just managed to get back to the flat in time, though the master key was still in his pocket. "And he asked for some more fruit too. Oh well, he can have it tomorrow, I can't miss another bus . . . Are you *listening*, Oliver?"

Bacillus, *bacillus*. What was that? He'd have to look it up in his father's big dictionary, when the coast was clear. "It can survive for months, even for years, if . . . if kept in the *dark* . . . curiously, the flea is very attracted to white objects" . . . half a dozen eggs, a large white loaf, and a tin of stewing steak . . . bacillus, *fleas* . . . two toilet rolls and a box of Persil Automatic . . . He must get it firmly into his head, like one of his mother's shopping lists, and the minute she'd gone out again he must write it all down, in his "dream book". Oliver didn't keep a diary but he always wrote down the things that were very important to him. Ted Hoskins' "attack" in their street had been important, so was the stone Geoff had given him. His dreams of Number Nine, way back in time, were important too. He'd written down every detail of those.

He smiled a little smile to himself as he climbed the attic stairs to his room to get his book out. So old Dr Verney didn't just think the house was overrun by rats and mice, he thought they'd got fleas as well.

What would his mother say, if she knew!

Chapter Ten

A couple of days later, before school, Tracey Bell pounced on him in the playground. She'd not yet managed to get herself into Number Nine while her mother did the cleaning, she'd been dumped at her Gran's; but she'd phoned Oliver up twice, and told him her Uncle Len was sending them a rat. Here it was.

"He put it in this for now," she said, and she pushed a small wooden box into his hands. It was smelly, and there was already a little hole chewed in the side. "This won't do," Oliver said ungraciously, putting it on the ground and eyeing it with suspicion. "It's going to eat its way out of there. Look, it's started already."

"But it's only for *now*. It can go in its proper cage when you get it home. You did *get* a cage, didn't you, Oll?" and Tracey stared at him accusingly.

Oliver avoided a direct lie by taking the lid off the box. He couldn't see anything at first, except a lot of wood shavings, then something moved underneath them and a little face popped out. He saw a sleek black head with quivering whiskers and pink see-through ears. "It's only a baby," he whispered, his fingers on the lid in case it decided to jump out and explore the playground. The tiny thing was quite beautiful.

"I know," Tracey said proudly. "Sweet i'n't it? And it's a boy, so there won't be any babies."

Well, that was something. One rat was going to pose enough problems. A whole family of them would give his mother a nervous breakdown. It had put two minute pink paws on the side of the box now, and its head was going from side to side, as if it was watching Wimbledon. Tracey stretched out a fat finger and stroked it. "I'n't it lovely?" she said admiringly. "Let's call it Roland, there's a Roland Rat on the telly."

"No . . . Rufus," Oliver grunted. He didn't want it called after something on T.V. and Rufus sounded much grander, it was a kingly sort of name. Anyway, it wouldn't always be so tiny, rats grew quite big. "I thought it'd be white," he said, "I didn't know there were black rats."

"Well, this is a fancy one. Rats *used* to be black, before we got brown ones, y'know, in the olden days. Uncle Len told me that."

It seemed to enjoy being tickled behind its ears and there was quite a crowd round them now, oohing and aahing. Oliver stretched out one finger and touched its head gingerly. He'd better try to make friends with it. After all, it was going to live in their cellar. But at that moment the bell went for Assembly and everyone scattered. Rufus dived back into his shavings, but not before he'd taken a sharp nip at Oliver's middle finger.

"The rotten thing!" he shouted, sucking his hand and slamming the lid back on the box. "It's drawn blood . . . it's vicious!"

"Don't be daft," Tracey told him, "it's only got its milk teeth. It's just being friendly."

Some friend, Oliver thought, following her into school. I give it a little pat and it takes a big chunk out of my finger. He would have to handle Rufus very carefully, and get to know him, otherwise he'd turn wild and never come out of his cage without making straight off. Kit McKenzie wouldn't want anything like that on her television programme.

During school Mr Jordan kept Rufus in the science lab. "It bit me," Oliver told him when he went in during the lunch hour to see how the rat was getting on.

"Let's have a look."

Oliver showed him his finger. There was a small black line on it, rather like a splinter, and the skin looked very pink and swollen. "Sore, is it?" the teacher asked him.

"Yes it is, a bit."

"You should have told someone, Oliver, and they'd have put a drop of T.C.P. on it for you. We'll do it now. Better late than never."

"Late for what?" Oliver said suspiciously.

"Well, it's an animal bite, and you can't be too careful. Wild rats carry disease, of course," he added vaguely.

"*Disease*?"

Mr Jordan grinned, and put a hand on his shoulder. "Look, I'm sure it's perfectly all right, but we'll just clean it up for you. Tell your mother about it when you get home. I'm sure you're up to date with all your injections, but if by any chance you're not, you ought to have an anti-tetanus jab, just to be on the safe side."

Oliver followed him down the corridor to the Medical Room, and stuck his hand out while the science master dabbed his finger with cotton wool. He felt distinctly queasy now, his hand throbbed and his head ached, and his stomach was doing somersaults. It was all this talk of infection and anti-tetanus jabs. He didn't know rats could carry diseases. No wonder old Dr Verney was so fussy about his bedsitter, no wonder he stuffed newspaper down those cracks in the skirting board. Perhaps he wasn't so potty after all . . . "The bacillus can survive for years in a rodent's burrow . . ." Weren't *rats* "rodents"?

"I've got a slight problem about this rat," he confided to Mr Jordan, when they were back in the lab. "We've not got anything suitable to keep it in at home, and it's going to eat its way out of this box." He was looking at an empty gerbil cage on one of the benches. Some nut had let the school gerbils out, one afternoon, and the caretaker's cat had eaten them. That cage would be ideal for Rufus. It had an exercise wheel and a feeding bowl, and a proper upsidedown bottle for water. "Could we borrow that, do you think?" he asked.

Mr Jordan had a look at it. "I don't see why not. Let's see if he likes it, shall we?" Before handling Rufus he took a thick gardening glove from a drawer and slipped it on. The rat was scooped out of its shavings and plopped quickly into the gerbil cage. For a few seconds it sat shivering in a corner, then, very slowly, it started to explore, sniffing at the waterbottle, and scurrying up and down.

"It's O.K.," Mr Jordan said, "but you'll have to get a bag of shavings for it, and some hamster food. That's what they eat."

"I know. Tracey's uncle sent me a book. I read it at break. It tells you exactly what to do." He peered into the gerbil cage, holding his throbbing finger straight up in the air. "It throbs less, if you do that," he explained to Mr Jordan. "It takes the blood away from your extremities."

The science teacher looked at him thoughtfully. Oliver Wright was the cleverest boy in the school, well-informed about nearly everthing, and with a photographic memory. That rat would be given the royal treatment because the boy would look after it strictly according to the rules. The puzzling thing was how he'd persuaded that mother of his to let him have it in the first place. She was an awkward woman, always coming in to complain about the way the school was run. Some of the teachers made themselves scarce when Mrs Wright called in for one of her "little chats".

"I can drop this off for you," he told Oliver. "It's on my way home. It'll be a bit awkward otherwise, won't it, taking it on the bus?"

"Oh *no*," the boy said anxiously, "it's O.K., honestly.

Someone'll give me a lift. I'll ask Terry Whelan's mum, they live near us." The last thing he wanted was for Mr Jordan to knock on the door with Rufus. That would be The End, and he was already getting quite interested in this rat project, in spite of his sore finger.

"Well, all right then, if you're sure. Don't forget to tell your mum about that nip he gave you . . . and good luck. He's a beautiful specimen, I must say. He'd look rather good on T.V."

Oliver was shattered when he reached Thames Terrace. He'd walked all the way, carrying the cage, but going through side streets and across waste ground, to avoid the school crowd. People were so interested in Rufus they'd started to follow him home. At one point he'd had to disappear into the Underground, to shake them off.

When he was three houses away from Number Nine he dumped the cage on the edge of the pavement, crept up to the brown front door and slipped into the hall. Everything was as usual. Mr Porter was snoring loudly in front of his television set and the sound of his mother's radio came wafting down the stairs. She was listening to a play about coal miners. He opened the door of the cubbyhole under the stairs, dashed out again, grabbed the gerbil cage and tore back. Before he could stop it the front door slammed shut. Upstairs the bellowing coal miners were switched off, and he heard the flat door open. "Is that you, Oliver? You're *late*!" his mother shouted.

"I know, sorry. We had a choir practice, I forgot to tell you," he called back. Well, he had to say something or she'd get suspicious. But she'd already started coming down the stairs. In a sweat he squeezed through to the back of the cubbyhole and shoved Rufus right up against the wall. Then he crawled out again, backwards, rearranging all the suitcases and boxes so that the cage was completely hidden. He'd just straightened up again, and flattened his hair down, when his mother's face appeared over the banisters. "You look hot," she told him, "and your face is absolutely filthy. What on earth have you been doing?"

"Oh, you know," he replied weakly. "By the way, Mum, I came top in that maths test."

"Well, that'll cheer your father up," she said. "Come on, you need a wash." Oliver sagged with relief. He'd managed to get her off the scent, and she wasn't going to ask him why he'd got cobwebs in his hair. "Cheer him up?" he repeated, following her into the flat.

"Well, they were going to send him home tomorrow, but he's developed some sort of chest infection. He's quite poorly actually."

It was awful of him but Oliver felt rather relieved – just as long as his father didn't get any worse. It was going to be difficult enough, keeping a rat a secret from his mother, but with both parents in the house it would be almost impossible. And his father had very good hearing. He always heard the click of Oliver's bedside light, for example, switched on after hours for a spot of illicit reading. He'd certainly have heard the regular little whirring noise that had started up the minute the cubbyhole door was shut. Rufus had discovered his exercise wheel.

It was late-night shopping that day and Oliver went for the groceries while his mother visited the hospital. She still didn't want him to go with her, this time because of his father's chest infection. Oliver wasn't feeling too marvellous himself. He was sweaty and hot, and his head ached. His finger was quite swollen now but he'd removed

Mr Jordan's bandage. His mother would pounce, if she saw that, and it would be curtains for the rat project.

The huge supermarket where they did their shopping had a "Pets" section so he bought shavings, hamster food, and vitamin drops out of his savings. He didn't know how he was going to get the drops down Rufus but he was determined to try. Uncle Len's book said they were necessary, to keep your rat in prime condition.

When he'd put everything away he went downstairs and pulled the gerbil cage out of the cubbyhole. Mrs MacDougall was glued to "Coronation Street" and Mr Porter was singing loudly behind his door. He'd obviously had an unusually good time at The Three Jolly Sailors. There was no noise coming from Dr Verney's bedsitter but whiffs of that peculiar chemical smell hung round, on the landing. He'd obviously got another of his "air fresheners" going.

In the cellar Oliver cleared a large space, well away from the grating. He couldn't put Rufus there because his mother was bound to come down, sooner or later, to inspect the cracks. Instead he made a little fortress of books and packing cases in the opposite corner, and placed the gerbil cage in the middle of it. To get through he'd have to dismantle everything, every time, but he just couldn't risk his mother finding out.

When he'd settled Rufus for the night, and restored the boxes, he stood by the grating and stared at the cracks. In spite of his aching head and his throbbing middle finger, and his creeping fear about "the darkness", he wanted to be taken back into that other world. He felt for the little stone, still on a string round his neck, and held it tight. Perhaps that would take him back to his dying sister Abigail, to grave-faced Elizabeth and to his beautiful, grieving mother. He looked hard into the black gashes in the wall, willing himself to be sucked back into the past again, straining his ears for that anguished weeping that had become so familiar to him. But nothing happened. In the dark Rufus trundled round on his wheel; the only other noise was a car being revved up along the street.

He couldn't sleep that night and it wasn't really because of Rufus – if his mother found out he'd just have to face her. It was because he couldn't go back. He wanted those dreams again, but they wouldn't come.

That other place was a world of great suffering and pain, a place where people were screaming and raving, dying off like flies. Yet he belonged to it, more than he belonged to his own world.

He woke up very early next morning with the definite feeling that there'd been an important "development" at River Reach. It was more than a hunch this time, it was an absolute conviction, and he knew that he couldn't ignore it. So the minute he was dressed he crept downstairs and slipped out to the demolition site.

He wasn't at all surprised when he saw all the police cars at River Reach. Although it was still quite early the building site was like an ant heap. Men were busy with orange cones, marking off big sections of the site, and a huge roll of thick polythene was being taken out of a van. That would be to cover up whatever they'd found. Perhaps they'd bring bags out next, plastic zipper bags to put dead bodies in.

He couldn't get anywhere near the excavations because everything had been roped off, and it looked as if they were getting ready to put up a much higher fence. A lorry had arrived with posts, and sheets of corrugated iron, and Rick was deep in conversation with two other men, kicking at the existing fence and scowling. A new fence meant the whole thing was "long term"; they wouldn't bother with that if the police were going to take everything away. And that roll of plastic sheeting suggested there was far too much involved for one van, for one day . . .

Quite a few people were hanging about, round the site entrance, but nobody went in because a policeman stood on duty at the gates. Oliver sidled over to him and pricked up his ears. "No comment," he was saying to a man with a notebook and a camera. "A thing as big as this will take time. We've got to call the coroner in first, I'm sure there'll be a press conference eventually."

A coroner. That meant human remains. Perhaps they'd discovered the three missing Gillet children; they'd disappeared two years ago, from a street very near Thames Terrace, and never been found. His mother had become much more fussy about where Oliver went after that.

Dr Verney was standing next to the reporter, clasping and unclasping his hands in that worried old man's way of his. He was staring down into the muddy excavations, then back along the street, at St Olave's churchyard, muttering numbers to himself, then stroking the side of his face, thoughtfully. He seemed to be counting. He still gave Oliver a creepy sort of feeling; it was his face. He'd never met Dr Verney before the day he'd turned up at Number Nine, and yet he felt he knew him. It was another of those "hunches".

Geoff Lucas had just roared up on his motor bike. He tried to slip past but Oliver stopped him. "They *have* found something now, haven't they, Geoff?" he asked him.

"Dunno, mate," the man said. But he did. The way his eyes slid away from Oliver's face told the boy everything, but he'd obviously been ordered to keep quiet. "They're always finding rubbish, you know," he added, as Oliver started climbing down onto the site, till a second policeman stopped him. But Oliver knew perfectly well that the police didn't waste their time on "rubbish". "Look mate, what do you want, for heaven's sake?" Geoff said, flushing with anger. "Some poor bloke's head? A body with its legs ripped off? You should get yourself sorted out, you should, you're morbid."

Oliver stared after him as he pushed past bad-temperedly. That wasn't like Geoff at all; something had upset him. "A body with its legs ripped off" . . . the words boomed and echoed in his brain. That was exactly what he'd seen in his "dream", except that it wasn't a dream, it was real. More real than real life.

But he couldn't get back to it, back to that terrible past where people went mad with pain and died. Was this anything to do with it? All these men rushing about, and the sheeting, and those two policemen on duty? Or had they just found the poor Gillet children?

Oliver stared down, along with Dr Verney and all the others, and a great weariness crept over him. It was hopeless now. Nobody would tell him anything, yet he had a strong feeling that somebody was being threatened by all this, they might even die. Was it old Dr Verney? Was it his father, lying sick in hospital? Was it Oliver himself? He didn't know the answer, all he knew was that he had to get to his "family" in the dream. If he couldn't get back, he could do nothing.

Chapter Eleven

The next time Mrs Bell came to do the cleaning Tracey came with her. She was thrilled, and her little round eyes darted about all over the place; she just couldn't wait for Oliver's mother to disappear into the residents' dining room, where they were planning to wash the walls down. She wanted to go "exploring".

"It's dead boring, living in a flat," she said, puffing and blowing as she followed Oliver up to his attic. "You've got tons of room here, haven't you?"

"Not really. Most of it's used by the old people. They've all got bedrooms, and there's a big dining room, *and* a sitting room. There's not much left for us. I bet this flat's no bigger than yours."

Tracey looked round curiously. "Well, it's different," she said. "Everything's a funny shape. I'd quite like this room, it's sort of, well, *secret*. Why don't you have Roland up here, Oll? It's nice and light."

"It's Rufus, not Roland," he told her, "and anyway, what are you talking about? I can't have him up here, because of my mother. I explained all that. I hope you've not said anything, Tracey, because if you have – "

"I've not, I've not. Only, well, I don't think it's very nice for him, being in the dark and that."

"Look, rats live in the dark, you nit, they're used to it. He's perfectly all right where he is." He was irritated. He'd got all the bother of looking after Rufus and, so far, it was going rather well. He'd started picking him up (with a glove on), he'd cleaned him out, and he'd even got the vitamin drops down him. All Tracey had to do was to plan what she was going to wear on the television programme, if they were chosen.

"Sorry, Oll," she said humbly. She got nervous when he lost his temper. There was something a bit weird about Oliver Wright. He talked like grown-ups, and she sometimes had the funny feeling that he knew exactly what she was going to say before she said it. "So sharp, he'll cut himself" – that was her mum's opinion.

"Can we go and have a look at Rol-Rufus?" she said. She was already bored with the attic, it was all books. There was no record player, no comics, apart from the ones she lent him, and no T.V. Perhaps she wouldn't really like a room like this after all.

"O.K." It was time Rufus had a bit of exercise and Oliver had managed to make a little run for him out of the chicken wire. "Just keep *quiet*," he told her, as they crept down the stairs. "No talking till I've shut the cellar door. If my mother hears us she'll ask me what I'm doing. Get it?"

Tracey nodded vigorously, and shook her pan-scrubber hair. Even so, she made a major production of going "quietly" down the staircase, taking great big steps to get to the cellar as quickly as possible, and nearly falling over in the process, then putting her finger to her lips and "shushing" Oliver. She seemed to think it was all a bit of a giggle. Halfway down he pulled her into the shadow of the plant stand. "*Listen*," he hissed in her ear, "we're in the danger zone now, they're in the room underneath. If you can't be a bit quieter we'll have to go back. For goodness *sake*, can't you make less noise?"

"Sorry, Oll," and she immediately changed to mincing little steps, for the last flight of stairs. But when they reached the hall she slipped on a rug and went sliding towards the telephone table. Oliver grabbed her and propelled her towards the cellar door. "Is that you, Oliver?"

his mother called down. "I hope you're looking after Tracey."

Looking after Tracey. He felt like braining her. O.K., so she'd got him a rat from her Uncle Len. Why couldn't she just make herself scarce, now, and leave him to look after it? "Don't say anything," he whispered frantically. "Just carry on, and mind the steps. They're steep."

Once they were in the cellar, with the door locked, he made her stand in the dark for a minute. He didn't trust his mother. She might be on her way down already, coming to check up on them. But the muffled sound of rubbing and scrubbing filtered down through the ceiling; she was attacking what she always called "London filth" with her usual determination, and no doubt giving Tracey's mum a run down on the oddities of her "old people" at the same time.

"Come on," Oliver said at last, "I think we're O.K.," and he started shifting the boxes so he could reach Rufus. But Tracey didn't budge. She stayed exactly where she was, at the bottom of the steps, goggling at him as he moved all the rubbish. She'd turned very pale suddenly, and her eyes were two little round holes in a white moon face; she was opening and shutting her mouth like a goldfish.

"Come *on*," he repeated, "You can get through now. Look at him turning that wheel, he's brilliant. I'll shine the torch on it." But she still didn't move. "I – I don't like it down here, Oll," she said, in a tiny little voice, "Can we go back upstairs?"

Oliver stared across the cellar. He couldn't see her face properly but she sounded a bit sniffly, almost as if she was crying. "All right," he said grumpily, "but it was you who wanted to come down here. What's up, for heaven's sake? It's not all that dark, and there's a window over there. Here, you take the torch."

"*No*. Please, Oliver, I don't like it down here, it's creepy . . . and I don't like those cracks."

"What's wrong with them? Never seen a few cracks in a wall before? It's an old house." His voice sounded perfectly calm and reasonable, because he was trying to kid Tracey out of her panic, but, in fact, she was making *him* panic.

Up to now he'd only ever been in this cellar with his parents, and that man from the Council, never with someone of his own age. Tracey was obviously picking up that same strange atmosphere which had so bothered him. She knew there was something awful associated with this bit of Number Nine too. She was young, even younger than he was, and Oliver knew that children were often tuned in to ghosts and spirits in a way grown-ups were not; he'd read all about it. Sometimes children even attracted ghosts to places, just by being there.

The odd thing was that Tracey Bell actually liked creepy things, it was one reason they'd become friends. The horror comics hidden under his mattress, which he read after "lights out" with the aid of a torch, all belonged to her. Last Christmas Uncle Len had taken her to the Chamber of Horrors as an end of term "treat", and she'd recently been boasting that her birthday outing was going to be a trip to a place along the river called the London Dungeon, and that was supposed to be the creepiest thing out. Yet here she was, in broad daylight, crying her eyes out in their cellar (she *was* crying too, he could hear her now).

"Come on, Tracey," he said firmly, rearranging the boxes round Rufus. "It's not very nice down here, I agree. If I can get my mother into a good mood perhaps I'll tell her, and he can go in the laundry room or something. I mean, he doesn't smell, does he?"

Tracey sniffed, and rubbed her eyes. "Dunno. I think

everything smells. I couldn't stand having to feed him every day, not if it meant coming down here."

"Why not?" said Oliver. It was important to know just what was frightening her. She didn't reply, but Oliver never took No for an answer. "Why *not*?" he repeated.

"Well, I just feel it's going to fall in on me and that."

"What's going to fall in?"

"The roof. I know it sounds daft but I'm scared I might, y'know, well, get buried."

"But what about the Chamber of Horrors? That's much worse. I mean, this is only an old storeroom, under the street. Look, you can see people's feet going by. And what about all your horror comics?"

"They're pretend," she said emphatically, going back up the steps, "they're only pretend, Oll. It's different down here."

"Nice woman, that Mrs Bell," his mother announced, adding more salt to the soup they were having for supper. "Marvellous worker too. She got through that washing down in no time, *and* cleaned all the windows. I must say, she's about one hundred per cent better than old Eunice."

"Old Eunice" had been their last cleaner, and a major disaster area. She lost things, broke things, never turned up on time, and always left the house looking as if a bomb had hit it. She was working as a barmaid now at The Three Jolly Sailors. Oliver's mother couldn't be more grateful, even though she disapproved of drink.

"Do you think she'll stay then?" Oliver said. He didn't really want her to. It meant Tracey getting all pally with him, and he didn't want that; he was a loner.

"I sincerely hope so. Why?"

"Oh, you know. I just wondered."

"You're invited to a party by the way. Tracey's, I gather. Here, she left this for you."

"Oh *no*." Oliver didn't get invited to many parties and he'd hated the few he'd been to. It was starting already. Why couldn't Tracey Bell just leave him alone?

The invitation was on bright blue paper and written in large, loopy handwriting. "Please will you come to my birthday treat at the London Dungeon? Meet 2 o'clock, Saturday June 21st, at London Bridge Tube Station. Tea in the Dungeon Cafe. RSVP."

His mother turned the soup down to "simmer" and read it over his shoulder. "The London Dungeon, what on earth's that?"

"I don't know, quite. I think it might be a kind of museum."

"It doesn't sound like a museum to me," she said suspiciously. "I shall have to look into this – if you want to go that is. *Do* you?"

Oliver hesitated. He did want to go, very badly. Terry Whelan had been twice and he said it was fabulous. It had scenes of torture in the Middle Ages, with full-size human figures, and a whole section on witchcraft, and people being stretched to death on the rack, and plunged into vats of boiling oil; it was right up Oliver's street. But he knew his mother would have other ideas.

"Funny idea of a birthday outing," she was saying, reading the invitation again. "You'd think a little girl would want to go to a nice film, wouldn't you? Or the ballet perhaps?"

"*Mum*. Can you really see Tracey Bell going to the ballet? Nearly everyone's been to the London Dungeon in our form. It's supposed to be absolutely fantastic."

"Mmm . . . I still don't like the sound of it."

"I'm sure it's educational, it must be, I mean, they take school parties and things." Oliver didn't know if the last bit was strictly true, but he did know that it was the only way to persuade his mother. His parents didn't have much spare cash but they always paid up for anything "educational".

"Go on, Mum," he wheedled, "I'd really like to go to this."

"Well, we'll see. Now eat your soup. I'll have a word with Mrs Bell when she comes on Thursday."

For the rest of the week Oliver was very nice to Tracey and by Thursday he'd got her well and truly primed. "The thing is," he repeated, as they parted company at the school gates, "to get your mum to tell mine how good it'd be for my *education*. She won't let me go otherwise."

"O.K., O.K.," Tracey replied moodily, "I've got the message." She was fed up of Oliver Wright, anyone'd think he was doing her a big favour, agreeing to go on her birthday outing. Perhaps the others were right when they said he was a bit of a snob. He was obviously dying to go on this trip, he'd been on about it all week. Tracey couldn't quite understand why; it was only a museum after all.

She'd better not show she was irritated though, or he might tell someone how she'd cried in their cellar. Tracey still couldn't understand what had come over her that day; she'd felt really embarrassed when she got home.

Chapter Twelve

Everything about the London Dungeon was black and creepy. The entrance was a huge black door festooned with spiders' webs and studded with black nails. Over it hung a big black sign: "Abandon hope, all ye who enter here", and there was a notice underneath that said "Do not feed the rats".

Tracey pointed to it, and giggled. She was at the head of the party, with her Uncle Len. He'd come to look after them, though he didn't seem too enthusiastic about it. Tracey had a frilly pink dress on and the frills made her look even fatter than usual. She reminded Oliver of a little pink pig.

He'd nearly not come, not because his mother was against the idea – Mrs Bell had managed to talk her round – but because he felt ill. The swollen finger had been discovered, and examined, and he'd been dragged off to the doctor. He'd said it was an infected insect bite and given him antibiotics but since then Oliver had felt steadily worse, stiff and headachy, and he'd been sick after breakfast that morning. He'd not told his mother though because she'd have clapped him straight into bed and that would have been the end of the London Dungeon.

Uncle Len's biggest disappointment was the "No Smoking" sign at the entrance. He'd already lit a cigarette at the ticket office but an attendant had lurched up immediately, out of the cobwebby darkness, and asked him to put it out. He got rather bad-tempered with the children after that. Tracey was a bit disappointed too because the cafe was at the end of the tour and she'd got money to buy sweets for everybody, to eat as they went round.

Oliver stood with the others and waited. He was itching to get away and go round the place on his own. He could see all kinds of promising things: an executioner in black, holding up a dripping severed head, and a witchy old woman plunging a stake through someone's heart. And the most spine-chilling noises were floating out of the darkness, muffled funeral bells, and eerie music, and terrible screams.

Uncle Len got everyone together and checked that some of them had watches. "I'm going to sit in the cafe," he told them. "This place isn't my cup of tea really, and you kids don't want me trailing after you, anyway. Stick together though, and I'll see you in an hour; half past three at the snack bar, hamburgers and chips all round. O.K.? Follow the arrows, and I'll see you later. All right, Trace?"

Tracey romped off to the first exhibit without giving him a second glance, taking the others with her; all except Oliver who stayed by the entrance barrier, watching her piggy pink frills disappear into the gloom. He'd told her he was going round *on his own*, if he went round at all. If he didn't feel any better though he might go and wait in the snack bar with Uncle Len.

He stayed where he was until Tracey and Co. had disappeared, "oohing" and "ahing", round the corner, then he made a start, opening his guide book at Page One. Oliver always did things properly. He read all the small print and he looked at all the details of every single item so carefully that after twenty minutes he'd only covered Early Myths and Legends and Saint George (whose tortures included "being tied to a cross, having his skin scraped with iron combs, being chained and nailed to a table, and sawn in half").

He soon realized, with some annoyance, that you needed a lot longer than an hour to do the place properly. It was all so horribly wonderful too; it brought together, under one roof, all the things he was most interested in: bloody deaths and tortures, witchcrafts and martyrdoms, and everything was so well explained, with detailed historical notices next to all the exhibits.

But it was definitely frightening, even though Oliver kept telling himself that the people in the carefully-lighted scenes were only made of plaster and that the blood was probably red paint. He'd like to come back with his father. Perhaps if he showed him this excellent guide book he might agree. Meanwhile, he'd have to skip a lot of it or he'd be late at the cafe. This was the last place he wanted to be left in on his own.

He wandered on for a while, guide book in hand, his aches and pains forgotten in the sheer awfulness of the place. It was Oliver's usual pattern, the place was scaring him silly but he couldn't tear himself away. The screams he'd heard at the entrance barrier had been getting steadily louder but before he could discover who was actually doing the screaming he saw the rats, a whole family of them, brown and fat, running about in a bright, clean cage.

Rats. What were live rats doing in a world of plaster faces and trick blood, a world where shrieks and groans came out of tape recorders hidden in the walls? When he turned the corner he found out.

At first he thought he'd gone back to their old house, in old London, gone back without that terrible roaring blackness sweeping him away. He could see his "mother" sprawled across a table, with a swollen black-tongued baby in her arms, and a girl that looked like Abigail stretched out on a bed. A small child lay huddled in a corner in some filthy-looking straw. Their eyes were all open and staring, with the lids rolled right back, and their flesh was covered with hideous sores. They were all dead.

The only person alive in the scene was a tiny boy; he was sitting in the straw with one hand stretched out, clutching at the woman's skirt, and looking into the darkness at the tourists as they shuffled past with their maps and cameras. Oliver stared at the lifeless plaster features, stared hard into the blue glass eyes, then let out a scream and dropped his guide book. *He was looking at his own face*.

"All right, son?" a voice said. "Here, you've dropped this. Not on your own, are you? Where's the rest of the party?"

Oliver opened his mouth to reply but his tongue felt like a piece of boiled leather. He'd got no spit and what came out was a croak. "I'm O.K.," he whispered, "it's just a bit stuffy in here. Perhaps I'll go to the cafe, when I've had a look at this, and get a cold drink."

"Good idea," the attendant said. "I'll come with you if you like, you look a bit pale."

"No, it's O.K., *really* . . . I just want to see this."

The man went off to speak to some boys who were sticking their fingers throught the rat cage. "Hey!" he shouted. "Don't do that, they bite. It could make you ill. Can't you see the notice?"

Oliver, still rooted to the spot in front of the dimly-lit theatre scene with its ghastly dead figures, heard the man shouting and buried his nose in his guide book. He could do funny things with his ears when he wanted to, make a singing noise start up in his head, a noise that blotted people's voices out. He was doing it now, he didn't want to hear about rats giving you deadly diseases. Rufus had bitten him last week and he wasn't feeling well. Now he knew what it meant.

"The Great Plague," he read, "originally called The Black Death."

Bubonic Plague first came to this country from the Far East in 1333 and stayed for 300 years, recurring every hot summer. It was carried by fleas on rats from the ships docking in London and at other ports, and quickly spread throughout the country, bringing terror and death to many thousands of people. The death toll for London in 1665 was 68,596, approximately one third of the total population.

When a member of the household contracted the plague, the house was marked with a red cross and shut. The family remained inside and were left to fend for themselves. Food was left outside the door. Many committed suicide rather than suffer the torments of the disease and sewed themselves into their own shrouds, ready for the pits. Day after day the disease claimed its victims and the city graveyards bulged with the dead. Stinking mounds of corpses, with only the thinnest scattering of soil thrown over them, became familiar sights to the petrified Londoners.

The first symptoms were shivering and fever, similar to those of modern flu. As the disease progressed, large red boils appeared on arms and thighs; the glands under the arms and in the groin enlarged; the victims had sneezing fits and vomited blood, often dying within three days. The progress of the plague gave rise to the well-known children's nursery rhyme "Ring o' ring o' roses / A pocket full of posies / Atishoo, Atishoo / We all fall down." Bunches of herbs were carried to cleanse the air one breathed ("a pocket full o' posies") and the "ring o' roses" were the plague sores.

Not until late last century was the connection made between fleas, rats, and their human victims, and different ages had different theories about the plague. In 1665 it was thought that the "sickness" was carried in the air, so that the plague doctors covered themselves from head to foot in thick protective clothing to avoid contamination. Their curiously shaped "gas masks" gave them the look of birds with huge beaks. At one time, fires were lit in the London streets in an attempt to purify the air, and each house had its "fuming pot" for the same purpose.

Nursing the sick, and disposing of their bodies, was a task for the lowest and poorest in society. Victims were often "hastened on" to their deaths, and their bodies robbed. The men who drove the death carts through the streets, ringing their bells and calling "Bring out your dead" would joke amongst themselves, even, according to one eye-witness, shouting out "faggots for sale" as they flung on board the bodies of small children. A grisly jest but who could blame them as, day after day, they broke into the sealed-up houses and found death staring them in the face?"

There was a lot more but Oliver couldn't read it. All the letters were wobbling, and blurring together, and his knees were giving way beneath him. Another party of sightseers trooped by and then there was a lull. He sat on the floor in front of the plague house and forced himself to look at that boy again.

The face was nothing like his, and the whole thing was in need of repair. There was a crack in one of the hands, and another, going up into the left leg. He could see places where the paint was peeling off too. Even so, he wished they'd turn off those tape recorders; there was nothing fake about the screams, or about the monotonous sobbing of women. He'd heard voices like that before.

Pull yourself together, Oliver, he told himself sternly, and he stood up, brushed the fluff off his jeans, and slapped the guide book shut. He wasn't staying in this place another minute, his head was throbbing too much; he just wasn't well. But as he turned his face away, he felt his head being pulled back, his scalp was being jerked about, and tugged at, as if he was a puppet on a string. The plaster plague boy was looking straight at him and this time he was opening his mouth; the hand that had clutched at the dead mother's skirt was stretching out now towards Oliver.

He screamed, shut his eyes, and fell backwards, banging his head very hard on the ground. But before the blackness came up there was the sharpest of sharp pictures printed on his brain. It was the face of that young boy, the mouth, trying to tell him something, except that it didn't look like Oliver Wright any more – it looked like old Dr Verney.

"I'm sorry your Oliver wasn't well this afternoon," Mrs Bell said, helping herself to another biscuit.

"He missed his hamburger and chips," Tracey added. "Devilburgers they were called. Good, wa'n't it?"

"Well, I'm sure it wasn't your fault," Mrs Wright said, but she sounded as if she thought it was. They should never have been left to go round that place on their own, it was irresponsible; Mrs Bell should have gone herself, not left it to Uncle Len. Still, she wasn't going to say too much. Tracey's mother was such an excellent cleaner.

"I'll pay for the taxi," Mrs Bell said, "that's only fair."

"Nonsense. He shouldn't have come at all. He'd been sick, you know, in the morning. Never told me, of course."

"What's up with him then?" Tracey wanted to know, chewing a biscuit.

"He's got a swelling on his hand, a bite of some sort. It's made him feel rather unwell."

"He's wandering a bit, isn't he?" Mrs Bell muttered, drinking her tea.

"What do you mean, 'wandering'?" Mrs Wright said sharply. She was getting annoyed now. She'd given the Bells their tea and she wanted them to go. She was more worried about Oliver than they realized.

"Well, he was saying funny things while we were getting him to bed."

"What sort of 'funny things'?"

Tracey tittered. "He told me he thought he'd got the plague. It was that thing in the museum. It was terrible. Me and Kevin nearly threw up!"

Mrs Wright stared at her in disgust. She'd eaten four biscuits and she'd spooned three lots of sugar in her tea. No wonder she was fat. Perhaps having Mrs Bell to clean the house wasn't going to be such a good idea after all. She was obviously a silly kind of woman, taking an imaginative child like Oliver to a horror museum.

She'd already had a good look at the guide book and she could see exactly why it had upset him. No wonder he thought he'd got "the plague", or whatever it was. He was never going there again.

"Well, toodle-oo then," Mrs Bell shouted, waving as they went off down the street. "Hope Oliver perks up. I expect he'll be as right as rain tomorrow. See you Tuesday."

"Goodbye." The door of Number Nine slammed shut abruptly and Tracey whispered, "I don't like her, Mum, she's just like an old witch."

"Shh, Trace, she's all right. Just a bit old-fashioned, that's all. Ugh, I wouldn't like to live round here, would you? All these old warehouses. I wouldn't like to come down here on my own after dark."

"They get vandals," Tracey told her. "Oliver said so. Did you notice their front door? Someone's painted a big red cross on it. It's the second time they've done that. She'll go mad when she sees."

Chapter Thirteen

"Now just tell me how you feel, young man?"

Oliver groaned, and turned his face to the wall. He hated Dr Binns. He'd got tiny screwed-up eyes and bad breath.

"The doctor can't help if you don't tell him what's wrong, dear, now can he?" Oliver held up his right hand. "This hurts," he said. "It really *hurts*."

"Well, there's nothing at all wrong with it. It's only a bite and it's responded well to the tablets. It's not even swollen any more."

"I don't care, it *hurts*, and anyway, I don't *feel* well. I keep getting these headaches."

"I see." Dr Binns snapped shut his little black case and went towards the door. "Well, stay in bed till you feel better, then we'll see. Goodbye for now."

The minute the door closed Oliver crawled out of his bed, knelt down, and put his ear to the floor. Their sitting room was directly underneath his attic, and he could hear people talking sometimes if he listened hard enough.

"Nothing at all wrong with him, Mrs Wright," Dr Binns was saying. "He's not even got a temperature. Is it school? Getting bad marks is he?"

"Certainly not. He's top of his class, always has been. Are you *sure* he's not running a temperature?"

"Positive. Look, I must go. Give him a couple of days off, and if you're still worried, bring him into the surgery. Sorry to hear about your husband by the way. I thought he'd be up and about by now."

"So did I. It's a chest infection, I gather."

"Let's hope that's all it is."

"I beg your pardon?"

"Oh, nothing, nothing. Only he's not a youngster, Mrs Wright, and these things have a habit of developing . . . still, he's in excellent hands. I'm sure you'll have him back soon."

Oliver heard the door shut, then the squeak of springs as his mother sat down in a chair. *So his father was ill too*, and Dr Binns hadn't sounded exactly cheerful about it. "The first symptoms were shivering and fever, similar to those of modern flu . . ." *Could he have infected his father*?

He racked his brains, trying to remember whether he'd been to the hospital since Rufus had bitten him, but his mind was a muddle, churning round with scraps of information that he ought to write down. In spite of his thumping headache he found a pencil and got his "dream book" out from under his mattress. He kept it hidden there, together with Tracey's horror comics, because his mother was a snooper. Sometimes she had what she called a "blitz" on his bedroom and when that happened things disappeared. She'd already confiscated his London Dungeon guide book.

He felt too feeble to write his usual neat notes, so he just scribbled things down as they came into his head. He knew about "bacillus" now, he'd asked Mr Jordan. It was a kind of spore, like the things mushrooms grew from, and it could live in the soil for years. That was why they didn't like digging up the graves of smallpox victims, apparently, just in case it got "active" again. "If smallpox can stay alive in the soil for years," wrote Oliver, "perhaps the plague can too?" And he underlined it. Then he added "fleas", "rats" and "doctors with heads like birds".

He was trying to remember what else that guide book had said when he heard someone knocking on the front door of the flat. He got out of bed again, stuck his left ear to the floor boards, and listened. It was Dr Verney, complaining that he'd just seen a rat on the landing outside his room.

His mother's voice was shrill. "Now listen," she said, "I've had as much as I can stand. We've been vandalized again – I expect you've seen the front door? And that's only one thing. My husband's still in hospital, and he's had a relapse. In fact, they're quite worried about him. Oliver's ill in bed too. I've just had the doctor to him. Don't you think I've got enough on my plate, Dr Verney, without you bothering me?"

She was shouting now, but the more she raged on the quieter and calmer the old man became. "I *do* understand, Mrs Wright," he said, and his voice was positively oily, "but I didn't imagine it, I assure you. It was only small, a black rat actually, but it was there. It went behind your pretty plant stand."

"Don't 'pretty' me, Dr Verney, and please leave my flat. I shall go and see the general secretary of the Society first thing tomorrow morning. I'm afraid I can't cope with your complaints any longer. A rat on the landing . . . how *ridiculous*!" and it sounded as if she'd slammed the front door in his face.

Oliver got back into bed and burrowed down. He'd come out in a sticky sweat. Rufus was small and black, he must have eaten his way out of his cage – and he'd been so careful too.

Could the rat have fleas? He'd not noticed any, but fleas were only little black specks – he'd seen them on Binkie. It was quite possible that Rufus was crawling with them and that Oliver just hadn't noticed.

He swung his legs out of the bed again, took his pyjamas off, and stood in front of his long mirror to have a good look at himself. A flea bite would be like any other insect bite, presumably, an irritable spot on the skin that went red if you scratched it and turned into a lump. Oliver's eyes moved slowly up and down, then he turned round, and tried to inspect his rear view. He was depressingly thin and scraggy, nobody would ever ask *him* to advertise coffee beans or aftershave on T.V. You had to be a sun-tanned six footer to do that. But at least nothing had bitten him, apart from Rufus, and there were no telltale swellings. Even so, the minute he got back into bed, Oliver started to itch all over.

Rufus could easily have fleas, and Oliver had handled him every single day. Rat fleas had carried the plague disease and you got it from being bitten. And he felt *ill*, both hot and shivery at the same time, his head was aching and his finger was sore.

Logic told him that the plague "bacillus" couldn't possibly have survived in the London soil for over 300 years, that he must be imagining things. "Mind over matter, Oliver", that's what his father would have said. But it wasn't as simple as that. After all, Dr Verney was a scientist and he was frightened about rats and fleas too. Just because it had never happened before didn't mean it couldn't happen *now*. Oliver might be the start of a whole epidemic, and Rufus might be the carrier.

The red cross on the door said it all. It was no earthly use his mother scraping it off and getting everything re-painted. It would come back again; it was the plague sign.

"Mind over matter, Oliver." The boy closed his eyes and saw his father lying in that gloomy hospital ward, nurses doing awful things to him as he struggled for breath, he may even need an oxygen tent. For the first time, Oliver wanted to see him. His mother had sounded worried when she'd spoken to Dr Binns. He'd said "these things have a habit of developing". If only he could visit him, he could see what was happening for himself. Then he could tell his father his theory about Rufus and the plague.

Mr Wright was a clever man and he'd always had a quiet, reassuring way of dealing with what he called Oliver's "wild theories". Ted Hoskins was great, of course, in his way, but brawn and muscle weren't everything. It was his father he needed now. He wanted to pick his brains.

In the quiet of the attic bedroom his little alarm clock tick-tocked. The noise seemed unnaturally loud, and Oliver shook his head from side to side. But it only made him feel worse, and he was so hot. Dr Binns must be wrong, he certainly did have a temperature.

He slipped down to the bathroom, found the thermometer, and stuck it in his mouth. Then he waited, three minutes exactly on his digital watch. He felt nervous when he took it out again, his temperature must be well over a hundred. But the mercury had stopped at 98.4, normal body heat. Oliver stared at it in disbelief, gave it a shake, and replaced it in the medical cupboard.

"Mind over matter . . ." Perhaps his mother was right. He did have a vivid imagination and if there'd been no Dr Verney, and no visit to the London Dungeon, he may well have felt perfectly O.K. Some things were facts though, that red cross on the door, for example, and the stone round his neck, and the shoes, and Ted Hoskins running madly down their street. Where did "facts" end, and "imagination" take over?

Later that night it occurred to him that Dr Verney might have "imagined" the rat on the landing, so, when he thought his mother was safe in bed, he went down to have a look at the gerbil cage.

He didn't dare switch the light on, in case she heard, or in case Mr Porter spotted him through the grating, on his way home from The Three Jolly Sailors. Instead, he shone his torch into the darkness and felt his way towards the pile of boxes where Rufus lay hidden from prying eyes.

The old man hadn't imagined it, the cage was intact, so was his chicken-wire "run", but Oliver had under-estimated Rufus's intelligence. The rat had found the weak spot, the place where run and cage had been joined together with fuse wire. Oliver had run out of it, so he'd finished the job off with very thick twine. Rufus had obviously gnawed his way through it and made off.

He didn't linger in the cellar, the dark was too thick. In the stillness it was like some wild animal, bunching itself silently, preparing to pounce. Oliver's feet were bare and he felt something run over them. He let out a shriek and the sharp sound echoed round him, bouncing back off the mouldy walls, and up from the flagstones. Was it a mouse? Or Rufus himself, perhaps, playing games with him? Or was it a huge spider, like the one William Briggs had in his bathroom cupboard; Boris the Beautiful, who was being groomed for stardom on Kit McKenzie's T.V. show?

He got back upstairs and into bed without alerting anyone, but his mother wasn't asleep. She was in the sitting room. He could see a strip of light between the carpet and the door.

On his way up to the attic he stopped and listened; an unfamiliar sound was coming through the closed door. For a minute he thought it was Susannah, his "mother" in the dreams, for whenever the blackness came, sweeping him back to the saddler's house in that dark little street, he heard her weeping for her dying child, for all the dead of London. But this wasn't Susannah, this was a thin, dry voice, half coughing, half sobbing, the voice of somebody who always fought very hard to control herself, for Oliver's sake. It was his mother.

Dad must be worse. She'd been funny about him at

suppertime, "holding his own" she'd told Oliver evasively, "no need for you to worry your head". But it couldn't be true, Dad must be very ill indeed, dangerously ill, even. Never, in all his life, had he heard his mother cry before.

Things were always worse at night. It was at night that the tiny niggling worries became great terrors. Death was the biggest terror of all, and death was in the air. As Oliver lay in bed, wide awake and thinking about his father, all his secret fears about spreading the plague came creeping back. Before he could stop himself, he was crying too.

Chapter Fourteen

Next morning his mother went out, straight after breakfast. She said his temperature was normal, and Oliver didn't argue. He felt hotter than ever though, and his finger still throbbed. He'd been ordered to stay in bed till she came back, and he didn't mind for once. She wouldn't let him go to the hospital until he was "better" and if he rested for the day he might start to improve. Besides, it was important to go through his "dream book" and to look at all the notes he'd made. He couldn't do that with his mother around.

She'd gone into central London to the Society's headquarters and she wasn't coming back again till they'd agreed to do something about Dr Verney. "Every time I phone they give me a different story," she told Oliver, as she got ready to leave the house. "Now that silly girl in the office tells me they've not even *heard* of him, she says they've no notes or anything. That's plain ridiculous."

Oliver didn't say anything but he'd once read a ghost story where the main character always disappeared, the minute he closed his front door and went inside. Yet again he started pondering about Dr Verney. His bedsitter was real enough, with those striped sheets from John Lewis's, and all the books, and he had the most enormous appetite. Mr Porter had complained because he always finished up the leftovers at lunch. Spooks shouldn't really eat hearty meals; it didn't fit.

He was still thinking about it, and reading through his "dream book", when he heard the front door of the flat being opened, and someone climbing up the attic stairs.

His mother must have come back for something, no one else had a key to their flat.

"Hello, Oliver, I gather you're not feeling too well?" the wavery old-man's voice said, and a black stooping figure edged nervously forwards across the carpet.

"Dr Verney . . . how did you get in?" It sounded rude, but Oliver was startled. He'd expected his mother's face, the iron-grey "perm" and the fussy blue hat she always wore, for going "up West", not this creased and crumpled old man, with his beaky nose and his small glittering eyes.

"Oh, you know," he said, with a shy smile, and Oliver looked at his hand for the familiar Yale key that opened the front door. It wasn't there. "I just came to see how you were feeling," he said pleasantly, sitting down on the edge of the bed.

"Er, a bit better thanks," lied Oliver. "I think my headache's going anyway. I want to go and see my father tonight, he's not very well."

Dr Verney didn't seem at all interested in Mr Wright's illness. He was concentrating on the V of Oliver's blue pyjamas; he'd seen the abracadabra stone, on a string round his neck, and he was staring at it. "Such a pity you won't let me look after it for a while," he said, in a wheedling kind of voice, and a knobbled hand crept out towards it.

"No, not just yet, I . . . I can't, Dr Verney." Oliver clutched at the stone and shrank back. Somehow, in spite of his thin, feeble body and his cloud of fine silver hair, the old man was a threat. The boy wanted him out of the room. It was as if he had brought the darkness in with him, even though the sun was shining through the window.

Dr Verney got up and wandered about, picking up Oliver's bits and pieces. "You've got a lot of books," he said. "You take after your father obviously, a real book collector you're going to be, I can see that already."

How did he know about Dad? Had he somehow got inside the locked study and poked round? Mrs Wright always kept their family affairs strictly private, and none of the residents had ever been inside Dad's room. Yet Dr Thomas Verney seemed to know all about it. "And what are these, Oliver?" he was saying. "My goodness, what are these?" He'd found the little shoes that Geoff Lucas had rescued from the skip, and he was examining them closely. They'd been hidden under his bed until this morning, but he'd got them out again to have a proper look while his mother was out of the way.

"You can still smell the leather, Oliver, that takes me back a bit. My family were in the trade, you know, for hundreds of years, tanners mainly. It's an honest-to-goodness way of earning your living, money in it too. I was the odd man out, becoming a scholar."

"You can still see the stitching," Oliver stammered, "where the needle went in and out." His voice sounded peculiar, cheeping and bird-like, the voice of a small child. And he was going back, here in the sunlit attic, with morning shadows dappling the floor. He could hear Susannah's voice, weeping in the plague house by the Thames, he could smell the smell, he could hear the rattle of the death-carts, see again the shadow of the awful duck man, spiky against the wall.

"They were buried in their shoes, Oliver," Dr Verney told him, staring down at the shapeless bits of leather, but his voice had tears in it now and the boy could not look at him.

"I know, and they sewed themselves into their shrouds. They jumped into the graves, didn't they, when the pain got too bad?"

"That is true, Oliver. All that is true."

"And that's why there's a cross on the door, isn't it? And that's why you've come. I'm right, aren't I, Dr Verney?" Everything was clearing now, like the early morning haze over the river that thinned and vanished as the sun grew stronger.

"Yes. That is why I came here, and why I must stay, in spite of the risks and in spite of the dangers." He was looking hard at Oliver now, with those penetrating blue eyes of his, and the boy stared back, and understood.

"I think you'd better see this," he said suddenly, feeling under his pillow for the "dream book". He knew now that it was important to show the peculiar old man everything. But when he surfaced from the bedding again, with his red exercise book, the attic was empty, the summer breeze wafting the curtains about, making rippling shadows.

Only then did he realize what had been "different" about Dr Verney. He'd stood by the window too, examining the tiny shoes, but his tall gangling figure had cast no shadow at all.

An hour later his mother rang up and told him she was calling in at the hospital before coming home. "Any luck with the Society?" he asked her.

There was an indignant snort over the telephone. "None at all. All the bigwigs are away on holiday, and that silly girl in the office says she can't do anything, she can't even find his file. And she's not allowed to authorize anyone to repaint the front door either. Well, as far as I'm concerned it can stay as it is. At least it will show people what I've got to put up with. If only your father were a little better I'd get him to – " Then the pips went and Oliver heard her put the receiver down. He rather hoped she wouldn't ring back, she was obviously in a fighting mood, and he'd got other things to think about now.

One was the local "free" paper which had plopped on to the mat a few minutes ago. The paper boy always left three copies because he finished his round quicker that way. Mrs Wright had often complained about it, she called the paper a "terrible old rag".

When Oliver reached the main hall he noticed that one of the copies had gone, and he'd definitely heard the front door bang as he came out of the flat. He picked up the other two papers and put them under his arm but before going back upstairs he opened the front door a few inches and stared down towards River Reach.

There was Dr Verney standing right in the middle of the street, glued to the newspaper. He didn't move till he'd finished reading the front page, not even when a van came past and hooted at him to get out of the way. Oliver watched him fold the paper, put it in the pocket of his trailing black coat, and set off towards the demolition site.

He looked at the front page before going back upstairs. The main headline was in gigantic black letters, "AMAZING FIND AT RIVERSIDE BUILDING SITE", and underneath there was a blotchy photograph of sour-faced Rick talking to a couple of policemen. In spite of the huge headline the article underneath was only about ten lines long. It said that something of "archaeological importance" had been uncovered at River Reach, that the site was now sealed off, and that, due to the nature of the find, no information could be made public until the experts had made a thorough investigation.

Oliver climbed the stairs very slowly because he still felt a bit dizzy, but his mind was racing. There was no point in following Dr Verney down to the building site. They'd never get past the policemen, and if it really had been sealed off there would be dogs too. He had every intention of going to River Reach, but not until he'd thought of a way of getting inside the new fence. For the moment he'd got to make another visit to the old man's bedsitter, now, before his mother came home. He'd got another of his "hunches".

Nothing looked different in the small bedsitter. The mattress had been stripped again and the stripy sheets were draped over the radiators as usual. He obviously removed his bedding every single day because of "the fleas". Oliver noticed too that the wads of paper stuffing the "rat holes" had been replaced with what looked like Polyfilla. There were big white blobs of it all over the carpet.

It was the box he'd really come for and he wanted to take it away to his room to examine it properly. But he was too nervous. Dr Verney might appear out of the blue, in that uncanny way of his, and find him tampering or his mother might come back from the hospital and find his empty bed.

He reached up, took the old box from its shelf, and put it down on the old card table. His fingers shook and his body was trembling all over. It wasn't the "sickness", it was nerves, and the horror of what he might see if he opened the lid.

Would something fly out at him? Would the air suddenly turn black with buzzing insects, blinding him, and sucking at his blood?

Would he find Rufus, a stiff little corpse? Or would the blackness come at him, the darkness he'd come to associate with awful pain and grieving? Lifting the lid might be like opening up Pandora's Box, and letting out all the sicknesses and sorrows of the human race.

He opened it but at first he couldn't look. In horror stories a box like this would contain a severed finger, or a single human eye, looking up at you. Books were one thing, but seeing such things in the flesh was quite another. But at last he let his eyes rest on what was inside. For a minute he thought there was nothing, then he put one hand in and felt the crackle of paper. He pulled it out and saw a sheaf of small yellowy bills, all stuck together.

Oliver took them over to the window and held them to the light. In spite of his fears he felt disappointed. Even if he could pull the papers apart – and they were so torn at the edges it looked as if Dr Verney had already tried – they didn't look at all exciting. They appeared to be accounts of some kind – he could make out little columns of figures on one of them.

He put the bundle down, felt in the box again and found something else, two bigger thicker papers that separated quite easily. Very carefully, using only the tips of his fingers, he laid them flat on Dr Verney's "desk".

The large, thick sheets were yellow and faded but the printing was still quite sharp. One was a list of some kind, filling two long columns. At the top it said "The Diseases and Casualties This Week". Then they were listed in alphabetical order.

"Aged" he read, and against it, "45", "Bleeding – 1." Then came "Broken Legge", "Consumption", "Convulsion", "Cough". One person had died from "Shingles", ten from "Vomiting", twenty from "Wormes". The number of deaths from "Plague" was four thousand two hundred and thirty-seven.

Oliver put it down and picked up the other sheet. At the top it said 'London's Dreadful Visitation' and it was framed in a thick black border full of little drawings, white lines on black. There were grinning skeletons, and grave diggers' spades, large old-fashioned egg-timers, and broken bones. At the top there was a much bigger

The Diseases and Casualties this Week.

Disease	Number	Disease	Number
Abortive	4	Imposthume	8
Aged	45	Infants	22
Bleeding	1	Kingsevil	4
Broken legge	1	Lethargy	1
Broke her scull by a fall in the street at St. Mary VVoolchurch	1	Livergrown	1
Childbed	28	Meagrome	1
Chrisomes	9	Palsie	1
Consumption	126	Plague	4237
Convulsion	89	Purples	2
Cough	1	Quinsie	5
Dropsie	53	Rickets	23
Feaver	348	Rising of the Lights	18
Flox and Small-pox	11	Rupture	1
Flux	1	Scurvy	3
Frighted	2	Shingles	1
Gowt	1	Spotted Feaver	166
Grief	3	Stilborn	4
Griping in the Guts	79	Stone	2
Head-mould-shot	1	Stopping of the stomach	17
Jaundies	7	Strangury	3
		Suddenly	2
		Surfeit	74
		Teeth	111
		Thrush	6
		Tiffick	9
		Ulcer	1
		Vomiting	10
		Winde	4
		Wormes	20

Christned	Males 90	Buried	Males 2777	Plague	4237
	Females 81		Females 2791		
	In all 171		In all 5568		

Increased in the Burials this Week —— 249

Parishes clear of the Plague —— 27 Parishes Infected —— 103

The Assize of Bread set forth by Order of the Lord Maior and Court of Aldermen,
A penny Wheaten Loaf to contain Nine Ounces and a half, and three half-penny White Loaves the like weight.

"The Diseases and Casualties this Week", showing 4,237 plague deaths out of a total of 5,568

decoration, a skull and crossbones surmounted with a winged hour-glass, and a scroll that said "Memento Mori".

He folded them carefully and put them back in the box. If only he could take them away to his room and copy everything into his "dream book". But he just couldn't risk it. Dr Verney might pop up at any minute.

The bundle of yellow bills ought to go back too, but Oliver was hesitating now. Something told him that this was the real clue, somebody – the old man presumably – had been trying to separate it out into single sheets. Why do that though, if they were just old shop accounts? Steam was the best way to get them apart, there was a lot of that in murder stories. Villains often used kettles to open vital letters.

He put the tin box back on its shelf, locked up the room with his mother's master key, and crept back into the flat. Then he went into the kitchen, closed all the windows, and switched on the electric kettle. Soon the water was boiling hard and the room was full of steam. Oliver found a pair of kitchen tongs and held the wad of papers over the spout, at arm's length.

Eventually, after refilling the kettle three times and scalding his hand in the steam, it worked. The papers were curling and sodden now but he was able to pull them gently apart and spread them out on a tea-towel on the table. But the bills were all hand-written and the steam had made the ink run. All the letters were blurring and turning into little black splodges before his eyes. Oliver felt frantic. In getting the bills apart he was actually destroying the evidence he'd become so desperate to find.

Then a single name on one of the bills leapt out at him. He snatched it up, rushed across to the window, and held it in the sun. As the paper dried out again bits of it came away at the edges and floated to the floor, but the dancing black letters slowed down and hardened again. Oliver read it a second time, just to be sure. It said "Verney".

"To Martha L'Estrange, Searcher", he made out, "Of St Mary's Steps, to examining for the Sicknesse:

John Verney, Sadler	33 years	2 shillings.
Susannah Verney	31 years	2 shillings.
Elizabeth Verney	14 years	2 shillings.
Abigail Verney	9 years	2 shillings.
Sarah Verney	7 years	2 shillings.

All of Church Passage, Parish of St Olave-le-Strand. All dead of the plague.

Signed: Henry Craven, Physician, this 19th day of June in the Year of Our Lord 1665.

"Thomas," Oliver whispered, letting the frayed scrap of paper fall on to the sunny window ledge. "Thomas, Thomas Verney. Did you die too?" Susannah and John, Sarah, Elizabeth and Abigail, all dead of the sickness . . . that witchy old woman with death in her face must have searched their bodies for "the tokens", and said they were dying. Then the duck man must have come, and paid her two shillings for each corpse.

But he remembered those greedy little eyes of hers all too clearly, how they'd riveted themselves on Elizabeth's silver frog, and he remembered her harsh refusal to free Abigail from the cords that bound her to the mattress. Had she murdered them? Had she smothered them with pillows, perhaps, then robbed their bodies? "Thomas," Oliver repeated helplessly, "*Thomas*. Did you die too?"

A terror was starting now, deep inside him, a terror like a scream, working its way up silently through his body till it could find his lips and force them open. *He* was Thomas, in the "dreams", and yet the old man must be Thomas, too. His actual name was Thomas Verney, and his family had made all its money in the leather trade, and he was terrified of living at Number Nine because it harboured the plague yet he couldn't break free.

Oliver picked up the bill and gathered it up with the rest into a neat bundle, then he found a plastic sandwich bag and put everything inside, sealing it carefully with a wire tag. He'd got to keep the air from it now. Important finds like this sometimes crumbled away to nothing once you let them dry out. He'd been told that by his Uncle Alex. He was a top archaeologist and worked at Edinburgh University.

He knew he ought to put the bills back into the tin box but instead he climbed up the attic stairs and hid the plastic bag under his mattress, sandwiching it between his dream book and Tracey's horror comics. If Dr Verney discovered that the papers were missing he would just have to come clean. But he didn't want to, not yet anyway, not before he'd another look at "the Verney paper" and searched through the others for some mention of Thomas.

•

Chapter Fifteen

It was nearly one o'clock and his mother surely couldn't be much longer. Oliver was determined to go to the hospital tonight, and if his father was feeling better he'd ask him about the Great Plague of London in 1665. He was better than an encyclopedia when it came to general knowledge. If their house came into it, or their street, or St Olave-le-Strand, his father would be bound to know.

He went back upstairs, had a quick wash, and pulled some clothes on. Then he went into the kitchen and got a loaf out. He'd make his mother some sandwiches, and warm the teapot. It was vital to soften her up and persuade her that he really was better. He wasn't going to tell her that he still felt shivery, or about his thumping headache. She wouldn't be able to do anything anyway, nobody would. He was more and more convinced that his "sickness", and his father's, weren't physical at all. It was because of what had been disturbed at River Reach.

He was rooting about in a drawer, to find the bread knife, when somebody said, "Oliver, is your mother in? I really must speak to her." He spun round, dropping the knife, and saw Dr Verney in the doorway. His eyes were startled and staring, and his fine white hair had bushed straight up, as if an electric current was running through it.

Oliver's thoughts flew straight to the tin box, and to the plastic bag stuffed under his mattress. "If it's those old papers, Dr Verney," he began, "I can explain."

"*Look*, Oliver," the old man said in a hoarse whisper, and as he stepped forward he pulled open his stripey "grandad" shirt, revealing a scrawny pink chest. "Something's bitten me. I started itching when I was in the library, reading the papers. I need some ointment to take the swelling down. Your mother's a trained nurse, I gather. I wonder if she could recommend something? I've been bitten all over."

He'd come right up to Oliver now, and he was still holding his shirt open so the boy could inspect the bites for himself. Among the sparse grey hairs on the old man's chest there were dozens of little red marks; one or two were swollen and angry-looking where he'd scratched at them.

"I-I don't know," Oliver said nervously, picking up the bread knife and retreating across the kitchen floor. "She's out at the moment, my father's not very well. The hospital are a bit worried about him."

"Your father too?" Dr Verney repeated, in a dead kind of voice, buttoning his shirt. "First you fall sick, then your poor father, now this. Everything's coming together, Oliver, I knew it would, the minute I stepped into this house."

"What are you talking about?" Oliver said rudely, hacking a thick slice from the loaf. "My dad's only got a chest infection. It often happens after a big operation like that, and you've just got a few midge bites, Dr Verney, and . . . and *I'm* all right."

But he wasn't, nothing was "right", and he didn't believe what he was saying at all. As he arranged grated cheese on top of the bread the actual smell of it was making him feel sick. Dad couldn't be well or his mother wouldn't have gone to see him in the middle of the day, and those *were* flea bites on Dr Verney's chest. He'd caught a flea himself once, from Mrs MacDougall's cat, and it had bitten him all over.

What if Rufus had been in the old man's bedsitter and

infected it with fleas? Something had definitely attacked him, and yet none of the other residents had complained. *The bacillus can live for months, perhaps years, in the warm dark of* . . . "Dr Verney, listen," he said, abandoning the sandwich before he'd put the top slice on. (If he didn't put the cheese away he was going to throw up.) "You know things, and I know things. I think we should go and – " but the old man had disappeared again, in that uncanny way he had. Oliver heard his footsteps going down the stairs, then a door slamming.

He'd been going to tell him about Rufus, and he'd actually been going to suggest that they went down into the cellar, to look for him. He was a greedy little thing and not used to foraging about for his own food. Oliver's theory was that he might creep back into his cage when he got really hungry.

If the rat was spreading disease it would have to be destroyed, and the first thing to do was to locate it and lure it back into captivity. Then he might let fat Binkie loose and see if he could catch it. If that didn't work he'd have to kill Rufus himself, with his own bare hands.

When Mrs Wright got back to the house at twenty past one Oliver's bed was empty, and so was the rest of the flat. On the kitchen table she found two slices of buttered bread and a little heap of grated cheese. The teapot was on a tray, with two teabags in it. Underneath she found a note. It was Oliver's writing, but very messy. It looked as if it had been written with a very shaky hand. "Felt much better," it said, "so have gone to return my library books. Today's the last day. Back soon. Love, Oliver."

But he wasn't at the library, he was down in the cellar lying on the floor, out cold, with a half-open packet of

Cadbury's Fruit and Nut chocolate clutched between his fingers. He'd found it in his pocket and he'd decided to try and tempt Rufus with it. Mice liked chocolate, according to Barry Ferguson in their form. Rufus might like it too.

But before he'd been able to move all the boxes, to get at the cage, the rats had come.

At first he thought those odd little flashes he kept seeing in the cracks must be reflections of some kind from the grating window. But as he got closer to them he saw that they were moving, that they belonged to living things.

The flashes were gleams of light on glistening eyeballs, and the eyes were the eyes of rats, huge rats, rats as big as men. One of them was coming out of the dark cracks into the cellar.

He screamed and ran for the steps, dropping his torch, his outstretched hands knocking against the feeble light bulb and smashing it into tinkling pieces. Up in the kitchen his mother heard the scream and thought it was a child in the street. She was eating a cheese sandwich and wondering whether to go to the library and fetch him home. If he was hatching a bug he shouldn't be spreading it.

The rat was crouching at the foot of the cellar steps and there was no way Oliver could escape without climbing over the huge, bristling body. Its black coat was rippling with fleas. They weren't black at all, but a very dark red, the colour of the blood they sucked from human flesh.

As the terrible creature opened its mouth the whole world turned crimson. Oliver screamed again but the noise was immediately cut off. He had already fallen forwards, into that bloody sea, and the jaws had closed behind him.

Chapter Sixteen

It was night and he was in the saddler's house again, in that stuffy upper room lit now only by three guttering candles. At first he thought everyone was dead except him. Sarah, Elizabeth and Abigail lay on the floor, side by side, covered with a single sheet. Their feet were bare and their long brown hair had been cut off. He knew they had died, even though their eyes were closed, because the three young faces were hideously swollen and discoloured, and because the smell of dead flesh filled the room, blotting out the smell of the smoking log in the grate and the fumes from the smoking pots.

It was too late for fuming to do any good, too late for lighting fires outside the houses, too late for prayers. His three sisters were dead and his father was dead too. He sat hunched over a rough table with his head in his arms but his dark, puffy face was wrenched sideways staring into the room. One glassy eye was looking straight at Oliver, not blinking even when the flies crawled over it. *Flies*. The air was thick with them. They buzzed round the four corpses and over a platter of mouldy bread that lay on the table, inches away from the dead man's face, and they swarmed in thick clusters down empty strings that dangled down from the ceiling, strings where meat had hung. They looked like ropes of onions, all moving.

His mother sat motionless in a chair by the grate, holding him so close he could hardly breathe, so tight he was unable to turn his head round to see her face. But he knew it was his mother because her smell was familiar to him. He could still detect it, warm and sweet and clean, through the terrible stench of death. It was as familiar to him as breathing.

But he must free himself from her. When people died their limbs set rigid like concrete. If that happened her limbs would have to be broken to release him. He looked down at the arms that lay battened across his chest. They were covered with plague sores and the left hand was so swollen the thin gold wedding ring had made a bloody cut, deep into the second finger. A fly buzzed round it and settled, and he saw the hand move slightly and heard a faint moan. His mother was still alive then, but so weak she couldn't lift her hand to brush a fly away. If she died he would be locked in her arms for ever and nobody would save him. They had been locked up in this house and left to die.

He leapt from the arms that held him, like a human frog, and scurried spider-like into the darkest corner, cowering away into the shadows on a soft, damp mound. It was a heap of human dung but, in spite of the smell, he did not move away. He was free and he was whole, his spindly arms and legs were filthy, his hair matted with grease, his finger nails grown into talons. But there were no sores on him, and no swellings. He was going to live.

Then something moved slightly, in the opposite corner, and he saw a figure in a chair, across the fire from his mother. It was a tiny grey figure, bolt upright, the witch-woman who'd watched over Abigail in her last agony. Now she was watching him.

She sat with clothes folded neatly on her lap, brown and russet cloth, his sisters' dresses. He could see his father's outdoor coat too, his good one with the silver buttons, and there were four pairs of shoes set out neatly in front of her on the floor. They'd always had shoes to wear because their father traded in leather.

Very slowly, he raised his eyes to the woman's face, and

saw something flash suddenly in the steamy darkness. It was the silver frog charm Elizabeth had worn. Now it hung round Martha L'Estrange's shrivelled neck.

He went cold. Would she take a knife and cut off his mother's finger to steal the ring? Death must surely come soon but this terrible witch-woman might not wait. And he himself was small and weak, that stringy old body of hers might be too strong for him if it came to a struggle. What if she smothered him with blankets? What if she strangled him?

He stood up and looked wildly round. Only a few steps across the room and he could get through the door, run down the stairs and escape into the street. He didn't know what he would do there, where he would go, but he knew he must escape. If the plague didn't kill him this old woman would do it. Then he remembered. They were imprisoned in this house and nobody would unlock the door until Martha L'Estrange gave them the signal.

There were noises floating up to him from the street, the slow clopping of a horse, and a bell ringing. Then a cheerful drunken voice bellowed, "Bring out your dead". "They have come, Thomas Verney," said Martha L'Estrange, and she was staring at him now.

Her voice was loud and harsh, mannish almost, not the croak of a feeble old woman, and she had taken a step towards him. He cowered away. "Let me go, Mistress L'Estrange," he whispered, "let me go, I beg you."

"I am old, Thomas Verney," she said. "I have nothing. I sit with the dead, and risk my life, because they will give me no other trade. I must buy bread or I too will die, and you, child, have nothing to give me."

She was coming towards him now with a bolster in her arms. He recognized it at once. It had come from the big carved bed in the corner, the bed his parents slept in. She could suffocate him, there in the house, and no one would know. His body would be flung into the death cart with all the rest, and she would add his name to the bill that the doctor must write out for her, "Thomas Verney, age 5 years, dead of the plague". Then she would share her fee with the gravediggers. He was to be murdered for two pieces of silver.

"Mistress L'Estrange," he said, "there is money. Let me get it down for you." At the word "money" the hag stopped dead in her tracks and looked at him keenly, her small, hard eyes glittered in the smoky candlelight, and her mouth dropped open. She was the worst of all the searchers, his mother had told him that. If the sickness did not carry her off she would live to get fat on her pickings.

"Show me," she said, but she still didn't move away, and the stained feather bolster was still held over him.

He took a stool and, reaching up over the dying fire, removed two bricks from the wall above and felt inside the cavity. Then he brought out three bulging leather bags, soft kid, beatifully stitched by his father. They held gold coins, his father's savings which were to have bought them a little house along the river in a quiet country place when the saddler had stopped trading.

In his heart he said, "Forgive me, father," but he could not bring himself to look at that terrible dead face. Instead he watched Martha L'Estrange counting the gold. She did it very slowly, like a man sipping old, rare wine, checking and rechecking before she slipped each coin back into its bag.

She was still counting when a man came up the stairs and burst into the foul-smelling room with his hooked pole. But the boy did not wait to see what happened next. He slipped through his legs and got down into the street before anyone even noticed him. And no one came running, they were too busy arguing over the gold. It had bought him his freedom.

*

In the city a bell tolled midnight though there was still brightness in the sky, even at the dead time. It was late June when it never got really dark. He was glad of it because there were no lanterns in the street any more and no one kept watch. Every house had its red cross and the legend "Lord Have Mercy Upon Us". Nobody was left alive at the saddler's house, except his mother, and she would be dead before morning.

From a doorway opposite his home he stood and watched. A man took a ladder, put it against the window of the upper room, and climbed up, prising away the planks with a crowbar. A second man took them from him and laid them on the cobblestones next to a big mallet and a heap of nails. Then the windows were pulled open.

His father was brawny, with shoulders like an ox. This was the last house the death cart would visit tonight, and these men were weary. Getting a brute like that down the narrow stairs into the street would take too long, they'd decided. The windows were the easiest way.

The corpses were passed out on long hooked poles and dropped into the cart. Nobody touched them and, as each body swung in the air, the men turned their faces away and puffed furiously on their little clay pipes. Sarah, Elizabeth, Abigail. The naked, blotched bodies landed heavily in the brimming cart like lumps of bad meat; they had swollen up like balloons now but the arms and legs were shrivelled and stick-like, and the three cropped heads had the look of puppets, three polished balls of wood, with glass for eyes.

It took two men to get the bloated body of the saddler through the window, and it stuck halfway. He could see his father, the face wildly startled but the mouth kind, as he always remembered it, kind even in death, staring down at the cart with its load of corpses, at the grass greening the cobbles, at the old horse stamping between the shafts.

There was a lot of swearing and argument in the upper room, then somebody spat out of the window, and jabbed at the body with his hook. It moved suddenly, fell through and hit the cart, frightening the horse which moved off with a jerk. Someone in the street grabbed the leathers and pulled it to a standstill and the others came out of the house, throwing their poles on top of the heap of corpses.

They left the place as it was, unbarred, with the street door wide open, and the cart set off along the street. He followed, keeping in the shadows, counting the doors with their red crosses. In the lantern light the red paint looked wet and dripping, like blood welling up from great wounds. The saddler's house, the Silk Merchant's house, Mistress Blackett's, the house of Matthew Pearson by the Church of St Olave-le-Strand. All were ghost houses now, and the little wooden church was sealed up too, its graveyard heaped high and covered with loose soil, giving off the unutterable death smell he remembered from his walk into the country with Elizabeth. It felt so long ago.

Ten, twenty, thirty . . . he was counting the paces as the cart rumbled along. They had left the church behind and passed down another street but at last the houses ended altogether, the horse was pulled up and the men left the cart; they were lighting more lanterns now and talking. Then he saw a brown bottle being passed from hand to hand, and he heard loud laughter, and belches, coming out of the soft summer night.

He crept right underneath the cart. There were at least a dozen lamps lit, and they might see him. The candle flames marked out a space in the darkness at his feet and, between the spokes of the cartwheels, he saw a huge hole in the ground. They had covered their last load with soil but they'd done the work badly; the earth was sprinkled too thinly, like sugar from a sieve, and he could see the shapes of arms and legs coming through it, hands sticking up, bloated bellies, a single crushed head with a long rope of hair twisted tightly round its neck. So many people, hundreds and thousands of people. Too many to count. Fingers, and faces, and clutching hands. How wide was this terrible pit? How long? How deep? He lifted his face and stared out, across the night, but he could see no end to it.

The horse moved suddenly, and one of his feet was crushed under the cartwheels. He screamed aloud and his thin child's cry rent the awful silence that had fallen upon the place as they undid ropes at the back of the cart. A flickering light was thrust into his face and someone grabbed him. "'Tis the Verney child," a man said, and the foul breath washed over him, turning his stomach. "He must go back, there'll be the devil to pay if he's found here," and he was pulled out from underneath the cart and shoved under the man's arm like a bundle of rags, his bare legs twisting and his long finger-nails scratching at the grave digger's face.

"But the mother is dead, surely? He should go to the parish." The voice floated across the pit, out of the darkness, and the boy recognized it. It was the voice of William Cole, the master printer. In the good times he had sometimes drunk ale with his father, in the saddler's house, and brought paper and chalks for the children to draw on. Now he spent long days alone in his warehouse, printing the weekly "bills of mortality", listing the plague deaths as they mounted, day by day, seeing tens turn into hundreds, and hundreds into thousands.

"She is near her end," the child's captor told him roughly, "but while she lives and breathes the boy must be returned to her. You know the law, Master Cole. Stand away, if you please, there's work to be done here. You break the law yourself, coming here tonight. No Christian soul should walk out while we do this work, as you know well."

The cart was turned round and the horse pulled slowly backwards till the rear wheels touched the edge of the gaping pit. The boy was still held tight but he'd stopped struggling and, as they pulled on the ropes and the back of the cart fell open, he opened his eyes wide.

The bodies were tipped down into the pit like beer barrels down a chute. It was like coal being heaved out of sacks into underground cellars, like potatoes being weighed out for market. They had brought a huge load and they were impatient to finish their night's work; they thrust their poles and spades into the cart to free what had been left in the bottom by jabbing and scraping. Even before it was empty a man had started shovelling earth.

He could see a tiny child, white and slippery-looking, like a fish helpless on a line, speared up on a man's pole then flung over his head, down into the blackness of the stinking pit. There was no priest there to pray for them, no singing black-frocked mourners, only the noise of the earth pattering down on the tangle of limbs and the staring faces, the grunts of the diggers, and the bottle being passed from hand to hand.

"Christ have mercy," said a voice, and the cloaked figure of William Cole stepped forwards, right up to the cart. He looked down into the pit, and crossed himself, then he stretched out a hand and touched the boy's face. It was stony, the small features stilled, as if carved from smooth rock, and his eyes were riveted to the eyes that looked out of the pit, the desperate, terrified eyes, now fast disappearing under a thin scattering of London soil. There in the pit lay his sister Abigail, his sister Sarah, his sister Elizabeth; there lay his precious father who had danced him on his knee in the saddler's shop. The boy opened his mouth at last, and gave a single terrible cry.

"Hush your noise!" and his cheek was stinging from the blow. He was now being passed rapidly from one pair of arms to the next, like something dangerous or unclean, but the last man held him. He was thrown into the bottom of the death cart, on top of the spades and poles, the horse was turned round again and the wheels rolled forwards. "Let me take him," he heard, "John Verney was my good friend . . ." But the men were adamant and the boy knew why. They had gold in their pockets now, he'd seen the three leather bags thrown into the gutter as the death cart passed St Olave's Church. If he was given to Master Cole he could tell him about Martha L'Estrange, and how they'd come upon her counting his father's money. What had they done to her? If they were proved robbers, or murderers, they would go to the gallows.

As they went back, past the churchyard, he stood up in the cart. One man was running ahead and, as the horse slowed down outside the saddler's house, he saw him ready at the street door, with the mallet and the nails in his hand. "Go to your mother, Thomas Verney," he was told. "She still breathes, she has taken bread from my own hand. May God spare you."

He crawled up the stairs in pitch darkness because the door had already been shut behind him and they were driving home the nails with great blows, making the whole house shudder. He stopped before he reached the top and lay there shivering. He didn't believe those men, they were evil. They had stolen his father's gold and they'd laughed as his body tumbled down into the pit, wiping the beer from their mouths. If he opened the door of the upper room he would find that his mother had turned into a grinning corpse. In the blackness something brushed across his face, and he felt a slimy tail. He shrieked, and a voice said, "Thomas, Thomas Verney? Is it my lamb?"

The door opened very slowly, and he saw his mother's face, swollen almost beyond recognition with the encrusted plague sores. But the soft voice was hers, the voice that had sung him to sleep so often. She had dragged herself across the room and now she was trying to sit up. He slipped past her and put his arms under hers, then he tried to pull her backwards so she could lie down and rest on the straw mattress, the bed where Sarah, Elizabeth and Abigail had died.

But he could not move her, so he crawled into her lap as she lay there, collapsed against the door. He wanted her arms round him while he slept so he lifted them up and brought them close, with the hands against his face. As she fell asleep her head lolled back and touched the door, and he heard the latch fall down again. They were sealed away here, nobody would harm them. The grave diggers would not return tonight and Martha L'Estrange would never return. She was lying dead in the hearth, with a gaping hole in her throat.

But he turned his face away. He would not look at that. He wanted to go to sleep with his mother's face in his mind; she was still beautiful to him.

He'd been dreaming all night, or so it felt, dreaming about the river, and the house his father would buy them in the country, dreaming of horses, when something woke him up. He was being shaken, and his mother's fingers were being prised away from his neck.

"Leave me!" he cried. But she was dead. He had fallen asleep with the slow throb of her body pulsing through his; now it had stopped, and the arm that had lain all night across his was cold.

"We are taking you to a good place," the man in the red

cloak was saying. "to a place in the country, a village where there is no sickness. Master Cole is waiting under the window. You will ride on his horse, Thomas, it's a fine beast."

"Why are you taking off my clothes?" The stranger's face was muffled up in his cloak, he kept it turned away from the naked shivering child, and when he carried him across the room it was at arm's length. There were no sores on the young flesh but the sickness hung in the air. Nobody knew how or when it started its terrible work upon its victims. Some said it was God's punishment for all the wickedness of men.

"We must go through the window, Thomas. We opened the street door and came up the stairs but we couldn't get in. The door was bolted. You were a clever boy, Thomas, to think of that, in case intruders—'

"I didn't do it," he sobbed, "it was my mother. She fell against it when she went to sleep and I couldn't move her. Let me go to her!" and he cried bitterly.

"No, Thomas Verney, hush now. There is nothing but death in the city. You are going to live in a fine place where they will treat you kindly. Take him, William."

He was passed through the window and lowered gently into the arms of William Cole, the master printer, wrapped round in a soft warm blanket and held close against the saddle tree. It was a fine saddle too, tooled and decorated with leaves, the best work of his father.

As the horse moved off he struggled, and twisted his head round, hoping to see his mother in the window, whole and unmarked, looking out for her children in her old way. But he only saw the man in the scarlet cloak climbing down from the house on a ladder, the shop door swinging idly on its broken hinges and the bloody cross, glowing red-gold in the light from his lantern.

Chapter Seventeen

Oliver woke up when something tickled his hand. He opened his eyes and saw Rufus sitting on his haunches, nibbling at a bit of Fruit and Nut. He looked thinner; he obviously wasn't much good at looking after himself.

He held his breath, turned over very slowly and suddenly brought his other hand down, squeezing the rat in his fist so hard that he squeaked. Still holding him tight he fished in his pocket for the new packet of fuse wire he'd bought to mend the cage, just in case Rufus turned up again. It was difficult doing everything one-handed, fiddling about in the semi-dark, twisting a bit of wire, but at last he'd filled up the vital gap between the cage and the run, and he was satisfied that the rat couldn't get out again. He'd have to disconnect the run though, it was too risky. From now on Rufus would have to take all his exercise on his wheel.

He was still sitting on the floor, in the middle of all the cardboard boxes, when the door at the top of the steps opened and the light switch was clicked on and off several times. "Oliver? *Oliver*! Are you down there? What's happened to the light?"

He got to his feet, swaying slightly and sick with nerves. This was It. He couldn't stop his mother coming down, and when she did she'd see Rufus. There was no escape.

A bright circle of yellow light came wobbling down the steps, and he caught sight of her tight grey curls, with the "up West" blue hat pinned securely on top. She'd taken the big rubber torch down from its hook behind the cellar door, and she was flashing it in his face. "I thought you'd be grubbing around down here," she said. "I met Mrs Bell on my way back from the library. She told me all about this," and she pointed at the gerbil cage with her torch. "A fine mess you've got us into, Oliver. Here was I, telling Dr Verney he was seeing things, when all the time it was *true*."

"Well, the panic's over," Oliver said. "I've caught him; he's back in his cage. Shine the torch over here, and I'll show you properly."

His mother wouldn't go right up to the gerbil cage but she directed the beam towards Oliver. There was Rufus, happy as Larry, trundling round and round on his wheel as if he'd never been parted from it. There was a very long silence, and he waited for the explosion, but all his mother said was, "It'll have to go back, you know, we can't do with it here."

He looked up at her, and wondered. Her voice was different, a bit softer than usual, and she was rather pink round the eyes. Something must have happened, something good. "How's Dad?" he whispered. That was what he really wanted to know, he didn't much mind about the rat going back.

"Better," his mother told him. "In fact, when I got to the hospital they'd let him get up, he was sitting in a chair. His breathing's much easier too. It's passed, whatever it was. I'm so relieved, Oliver . . ." and her voice petered out.

He got to his feet and pushed through the heap of boxes to reach her. "Come on, Mum," he said awkwardly, putting his arm through hers. If they weren't careful she'd start crying in a minute and he was no good at that sort of thing. "I knew he'd be O.K.," he said, following her up the steps. "Perhaps he'd just got what I'd got. Dr Binns said it was a kind of virus."

"Oh, they always say that, when they don't know what's

wrong," his mother said sniffily, sounding rather more like her usual self. "I've not got much faith in doctors."

"Well, *I'm* feeling much better anyway," he told her, "so can I come to the hospital tonight?"

"Yes, I don't see why not – you certainly look better. Your father's keen to come home now, though. Can you guess why?"

"Er . . . to catch up on *The Street*?" he said daringly. His father sometimes slipped out of the flat and watched *Coronation Street* with Mrs MacDougall. His mother didn't approve at all but Dad said it was his one bit of "relaxation".

"*No*, of *course* not. Don't be flippant, Oliver. It's because of what they've found at River Reach. Your Uncle Alex is advising on it, apparently. They brought him down from Edinburgh, specially. He's already been to visit your father and he's coming again tonight. You might see him."

"*Uncle Alex*?" Oliver couldn't believe it. He'd only met him three or four times in his whole life but he'd always had a special warm feeling about him. He wrote very funny letters and sent odd presents, joke books and disguise outfits and, once, a five pound note inside an Easter egg. The best thing was the kitten he left on their doorstep, one Christmas Eve. Oliver hadn't been allowed to keep that, Binkie had been there first and he'd chased it all over the house . . . But *Uncle Alex*, at the *building site*.

"Do you think he could get me permission to look at the excavations, Mum?" he said. He still couldn't quite believe it.

"Well, I don't know, he's not in charge of it, they've just called him in for his opinion. I don't think he's down for very long."

"Can he stay with us? I could ask him about it then."

"He's staying at his club, Oliver, like he always does, and I've told you, he's only here for a day or so, we can't really go asking him special favours."

"It's a plague pit, isn't it?" Oliver said suddenly. "That's why St Olave's churchyard's so high up. It's all the bodies they buried there." His uncle, giving expert advice at River Reach . . . it was a miracle. He'd been trying to work out how he could get himself inside that fence, he'd thought he might end up climbing over at night, and somehow get himself past the dogs, but he'd not really wanted to. He could be a bit of a coward at times. But if Uncle Alex told them that Oliver was his nephew, and that he'd just come for a quick look, before everything was taken away, they might let him through for a minute.

"How do you know it's something to do with the plague?" his mother said sharply. He was absolutely right, she'd heard her husband talking to Alex about it in the hospital that morning. But it hadn't been made public yet, and there'd been nothing much in the papers.

"I just know," replied Oliver mysteriously.

His mother glanced at him as they reached the front door of the flat. She didn't really understand her young son, even though they'd adopted him when he was only a few weeks old. What could his real parents have been like? She'd never been able to find out very much about them. If she had, would she have discovered that they were "deep" sort of people, like him? The sort of people that gave you the uncanny feeling they knew all about you before you actually said anything? She was fifty, too old to be Oliver's mother, but she sometimes felt he was the adult and she the child. "Old head on young shoulders, Mrs Wright" – that was Mrs MacDougall's view of him.

"Did the painter come and see you this morning?" she

said, opening a tin of soup for him and switching the grill on for toast. She was relieved to hear he was hungry. He really must be on the better side if he wanted food.

"No. Nobody came. Why?"

"Well, they've redone the front door, and after that stupid girl at the office saying she couldn't authorize it. I give up on that lot, they tell you one thing and they go and do quite the opposite. Anyway, I'm not complaining, I wanted it done. If only we could give Dr Verney his marching orders I'd feel one hundred per cent happier all round. But he's "dying" apparently, that's the latest. He won't get out of bed. He's convinced that something's bitten him and that it's given him an infection. Well, I told him straight, it's all in the mind Dr Verney, I said. I made him take his shirt off too; there were no bites, needless to say. He's got a skin like a baby."

She stopped to draw breath, and stirred the soup vigorously. Oliver opened his mouth to reply then shut it again. So the red cross had gone from the door, and the "flea bites" had gone too. It was the beginning of the unmaking, of time present and time past moving towards each other and becoming one. Soon Dr Verney would go too and there would be nothing left of him, no "Verney file" at the Society's offices, no mysterious daughter on the end of a phone, no letters coming through the door addressed to him. The spirit of the plague child was in the old man, he *was* that child, the child whose body Oliver himself had inhabited, in his "dreams".

But Thomas had not died, his name wasn't on the bill with all the others. He'd been taken from the arms of his dead mother and carried away to the country by a man on a huge black horse. Oliver must go and tell the terrified old man, he would rest easy then. The whole complicated puzzle had come together with excruciating slowness, as dream followed dream, but it was nearly finished now.

The fate of little Thomas Verney was the very last piece of all.

He went upstairs to his room but when he felt under the mattress for the plague bills all he found were Tracey's horror comics and an empty polythene bag. He looked everywhere but the wad of yellow paper had vanished. If his mother had been snooping she'd have confronted him with the comics and asked what the plastic bag was doing there. Perhaps the old man had been up here himself, and taken the bills away; they were his, after all. But if he'd done that he'd have *seen* the Verney death list for himself and he wouldn't now be lying in his bedsitter, waiting to die.

Oliver heard the phone ring down below, then a brief conversation. Then his mother called up the stairs, "You're in luck, young man. I'm not at all sure I should have said yes, really, but you've got your father to thank. He knew you'd be interested so he fixed it up."

"What are you talking about, Mum?" and Oliver clattered down the stairs into the sitting room.

"That's no way to talk to me."

"Sorry." He'd not been thinking, he'd been too busy wondering what to do about old Dr Verney.

"Well, do you want to go or not? Your uncle will wait for you, but not all day. He's going back to Edinburgh tomorrow morning. You've got to go now. Tell them who you are – and don't *touch* anything."

"Where? I still don't know what you're talking about."

"Uncle Alex, at the demolition site."

"River Reach? Can I *go*?"

"I think that's what I said, but only for a minute and don't – "

But Oliver was already running down the stairs.

Chapter Eighteen

The pit wasn't open to the sky. They'd put a great brown tarpaulin over it, held up by rough posts. He was allowed to climb right down into the building excavations and stand on the very edge. Nobody took much notice of him. There was just one bored-looking policeman, sitting on a stool by the entrance, and in the little hut where the builders made their tea he saw an elderly man in a brown suit, shuffling through piles of paper at a make-shift desk.

It was only half past three but the site was uncannily quiet. None of the machinery was in operation and he couldn't see a single member of the demolition squad. Uncle Alex explained that it had proved impossible for any of them to carry on, once the pit had been discovered, so they'd been moved to another job. "But we won't be much longer," he said. "There's nothing unusual about this, you see. It's a bit boring really. And, of course, the general public stopped hanging round as soon as they realized there was nothing worth stealing. It's only a load of old bones, after all, and they can see worse than that any day on the telly. That's the twentieth century for you."

"Don't you think it's interesting though? Oliver said, in a small voice. How could his uncle be so matter-of-fact about it? Was that what happened when you dealt with this sort of thing every day? Was it like doctors, getting used to it when people kept dying?

"Well, yes, of course it's interesting, Oliver," and his uncle looked at him thoughtfully, rather wishing he'd not agreed to let him come. His father had been very keen on it though, said the boy was interested in antiquities and all that. But he seemed upset, even though the remains in the pit no longer bore the faintest resemblance to human beings. "All I mean," he went on, selecting his words with care, "is that this is only one of many, Oliver. There are burial pits all over London and you tend to find the same pattern when you open them up. I didn't really mean 'boring'."

"I'm glad about that," Oliver muttered, and his throat had gone so tight suddenly he could hardly get the words out, they were like sharp stones in his throat. He wanted to be left alone for a minute. But his uncle, realizing that he'd taken offence for some reason, was very anxious to explain.

There was a metal ladder propped against the side of the pit and he'd climbed down it and started removing various plastic covers. "Shoes," he called up cheerfully, pointing to a heap of shapeless black lumps. "The grave diggers didn't bother to remove them, though the bodies were always stripped of anything valuable, of course, so you rarely find gold or silver objects in a pit of this kind." He replaced one piece of sheeting and lifted up a second, then a third. Oliver saw a pile of human skulls, all numbered and arranged in a neat pyramid, like melons at the greengrocer's, then rows of leg bones and arm bones, stacked together like firewood, and graded according to size.

"How many people would they have buried here?" he said as the bones disappeared under the sheeting.

His uncle shrugged. "Impossible to say, but in the hundreds, probably. St Olave's was a big parish, you can see that from the height of the graveyard. It's positively bulging. This pit took the overflow."

Oliver winced, and closed his eyes. "Overflow" reminded him of pipes and plumbers. The archaeological team had only gone down a few layers but the surface of the pit was fine soil, and faintly bumpy. He could see dismembered bodies, thousands upon millions of them, moiling and toiling round in a kind of vast drain, hands knocking against heads, knees against faces, all sucked helplessly away on a great river, the voices deadening at last into silence. That was death, a great darkness, and he felt the weight of it, relentless and unanswerable. Ted Hoskins had felt it first, sweeping up from the choked ground, and suffocating him. Here it was again, at his feet.

"Well, that's it, really," Uncle Alex said, climbing back up the ladder. "It just keeps on going down, all higgledy-piggledy. They didn't say any prayers over the poor creatures, I'm afraid. They just bunged them all in and shovelled the earth on top. And there weren't any coffins, of course. These were all poor people. Pretty awful, wasn't it?"

Oliver didn't answer but he pressed his lips together. All he wanted to do was to scream, and to go on screaming. His mother was buried here, in this terrible pit, and his three sisters, and the saddler who had danced him on his knee. They were his family and he wanted to be on his own with them.

"I'm going to brew some tea before I go," his uncle said. "Dr Manley's been in that damp little hut all day, writing reports, he could do with some. Do you fancy a cup? You could come and meet him. He's an interesting old chap, he's in my department."

"In a minute."

"See you in the hut then. The builders left us their stove but it takes a while to get it going."

It had started to rain and there was now a gentle pattering on the tarpaulin roof. Oliver thought of Rufus, scurrying over his hand in the dark of the cellar, and of Dr Verney shut up in his room, in terror of dying. He ought to go to him at once, tell him nothing bad would happen now, that it was all right. But when he looked down again, into the pit, he found he couldn't move. Death, which had always flirted with him in dreams and stories, held him still.

The rain thickened and the faint pitter-patter turned gradually into a steady drumming. Oliver wanted to rip the tarpaulin away and expose the raw red soil to the weather. He wanted the water to pour down into the open grave at his feet, washing and washing at its cargo of dead souls till he could see them all. He had played with horror all his life, poring secretly over grisly stories up in his attic, gobbling up all the nastiest murder cases in the newspapers. But death had always been what happened to other people, something he could shut away for the night, like closing a book. It was different now. If the skulls and legs and arm bones, all neatly numbered under their neat sheets, could be brought together again, they would turn into people, and here in the earth there were hundreds more. Every single one of them had once been a child, like him, and someone had loved them. When he thought of it, Oliver began to weep.

The rain was hurtling down now, and the wind had started tugging at the tarpaulin. His tears were coming so fast that the water blinded his eyes. He shut them very tight but the silent dead still moved endlessly across his vision. He was seeing, not merely the dead of London, and of the terrible plague time, but that great multitude no man could number. All the dead of history.

A cry broke from him at last, a real cry of anguish, not a child crying but a man. In his horror books he'd seen plenty of graves and coffins but in those stories nobody wept as the dead were lowered into the ground.

He stood there for a long time, a small thin figure plucked at by the wind, weeping for the dead of the years that had passed, and for those still unborn; for all the people who had ever loved each other, and been parted by death, and for all the human tears that had ever been shed.

When he went to bed that night he slept very deeply but he woke up with a jerk, while it was still quite dark, feeling wide awake and as if he was going on a very long journey.

The noise that had woken him was so faint at first that he decided he must have dreamed it. But there'd been no dreams that night and he'd gone off to sleep very suddenly, falling forwards into soft blackness. He swung his legs out of the bed and listened again. It was the woman's voice. As he crept down the stairs and through the front door of the flat he could hear it gradually getting louder.

He'd put his mother's master key into his pyjama pocket but he didn't need it. Dr Verney's door was propped open by a big glass paperweight. And he wasn't in bed, he was sitting bolt upright in a chair, muffled in a brown striped dressing gown. He was very pale and his papery skin looked damp. His eyes were round and bulging and his mouth hung open. Oliver thought of the skeleton faces, down in the pit. "You must come with me, Dr Verney," he said firmly, and he went straight across the room and helped him up out of the chair.

The old man didn't resist. It was as if he'd been waiting. He let Oliver guide him through the door and down the staircase. "Watch where you put your feet," he said. "I'll shine the torch for you," and they went down together, trembling step by trembling step, the old man and the child, down towards the cellar under the sleeping house.

Then Dr Verney stopped dead. "What's that noise, Oliver?" he said. "I can hear somebody crying."

They were nearly in the hall now, but he suddenly collapsed into a heap, shaking his head and spreading his knotted fingers over his face. "Let me go back," he pleaded, in an agonized whisper. "It's too late for me now. I can't go any further, I have no strength. There are rats waiting for me, great rats in the darkness," and he sobbed like a baby.

"All shall be well, Thomas Verney. All manner of things shall be well," and Oliver prised at the shaking fingers and held the hands tight. But the words were not his and neither was the voice. It was full and deep, and it spoke with authority.

"It is full of darkness," the old man whimpered. "I'm frightened of the darkness, I cannot go down."

"There is no darkness, Thomas, there is only light . . . and she is waiting for you. Listen, she's crying."

The boy looked steadily into the old man's eyes, and he saw them change. Fine-veined and bloodshot, a tired blue, they became fuller and clearer, the dark-brown eyes of a brown-haired child. The old man stared back and saw Oliver's own eyes grow pale, and the lines of time wrinkle round them. The man had turned into the child, the child had turned into the man. He got up, still holding on to Oliver's arm, walked with him across the hall, and waited for the cellar door to be unlocked.

"I can't go any further," the boy said, "but take this. It belongs to you. Goodbye, Thomas Verney." The old man bent his head and the cord was slipped over it, the string with the magic stone on, to ward off evil.

Oliver pushed the door open and the familiar, weeping voice swelled up out of the darkness. He watched the stooped, thin figure go down the steps then he turned away. He couldn't follow him into the cellar; he didn't belong to that world any more.

Yet he couldn't help hearing and, as he stood in the hall, his heart gladdened inside him. He had heard the woman's voice, how the anguished moaning had faded suddenly and died away and a new sound, a shout of simple joy, ringing through the house like bells. Then there was a cheerful babble of a tiny child, restored to its mother again after long parting.

Day was coming. The square of glass over the heavy front door had turned from black to grey. When his mother went in to see Dr Verney she would find him gone, the floor swept, the sheets folded, nothing left to tell her the strange old man had ever existed.

He put one foot on the stairs to go up, but even now he didn't want to leave. If only Susannah would speak, come out of the dreams and speak to him. He was lonely now.

But nothing broke the silence until the birds started singing in the oak tree outside the door. Then he heard a familiar rumble under his feet as the first train of the day left London Bridge station.

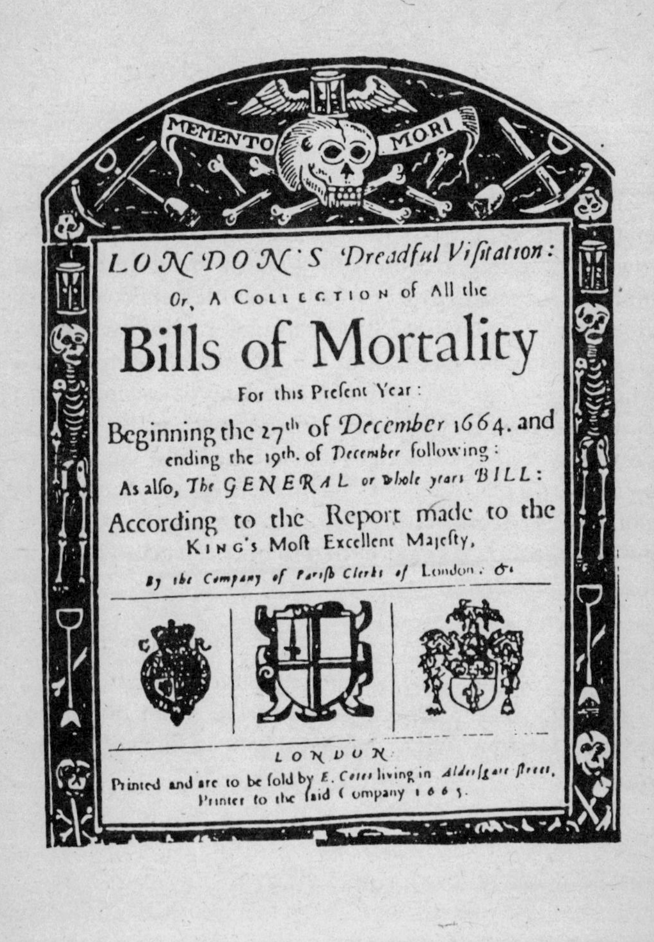
MEMENTO MORI

LONDON'S Dreadful Visitation:

Or, A COLLECTION of All the

Bills of Mortality

For this Present Year:

Beginning the 27th of December 1664. and
ending the 19th. of December following:

As also, The GENERAL or whole years BILL:

According to the Report made to the
KING's Most Excellent Majesty,

By the Company of Parish Clerks of London. &c.

LONDON:

Printed and are to be sold by E. Cotes living in Aldersgate street,
Printer to the said Company 1665.

From the Pages of History

On September 3rd 1665 Samuel Pepys wrote in his diary:
"Among other stories one was very passionate, methought, of a complaint brought against a man in the towne for taking a child from London from an infected house. Alderman Hooker told us it was the child of a very able citizen in Gracious Street, a saddler, who had buried all the rest of his children of the plague, and himself and wife now being shut up and in despair of escaping, did desire only to save the life of this little child; and so prevailed to have it received stark-naked into the arms of a friend, who brought it (having put it into fresh new clothes) to Greenwich; where upon hearing the story, we did agree it should be permitted to be received and kept in the town."

On December 4th 1665 Smyth's Obituary records:
"Cole, the printer, having survived the worst months of Plague, became distracted, and hanged himself in his warehouse."

Afterword

Thames Terrace is not a real street and Oliver Wright not a real boy but his "dreams" of plague-infested London in 1665 are taken from life.

The bubonic plague, transmitted by fleas that bred in the fur of the black rat, raged through the city for over a year and killed more than a third of the entire population. When the disease was at its height London was a ghost city, its thoroughfares and markets deserted, grass growing in the streets. The surest way to escape death was to flee, and thousands did, including the king and his court, but flight was not an option open to the poor.

Doctors and priests stayed on to minister to the victims. So did Samuel Pepys, recording the people's sufferings most movingly in his diaries. But the plague produced villains as well as heroes. The "searchers" who watched over the dying and certified them dead, the drivers of the death carts and the diggers of graves were amongst the most desperate in society. There is proof that the corpses were often robbed, and the sufferers hastened to their end by those with an eye to their possessions.

The way plague was transmitted was not discovered till the 1890s. In 1665 it was thought the disease was carried "on the air". Doctors covered themselves in thick protective clothing and carried herbs (a "pocket full of posies") to ward off "the sickness". Quacks and charlatans cashed in on the fears of the terrified Londoners, selling them charms and amulets, like Oliver's "abracadabra stone". The practice of sealing up whole families when plague was discovered drove people to desperate measures. The blowing up of the watchman, described in this book, is true; so is the account of the man who tried to save himself by swimming across the Thames.

The horrors of the time, like the horrors of war, produced its own stories of heroism and courage. The most tragic, perhaps, is that of Cole the printer, driven to suicide by the ever-increasing numbers of dead, recorded week by week in his "bills of mortality". By contrast, the rescue of the saddler's son, which Samuel Pepys described in his diary, must be the most heart-warming of all "plague stories", and it was that story which inspired this book.

A.C.

Black Harvest

Ann Cheetham

A chilling story of terror and suspense . . .

The west coast of Ireland seems a perfect place for a holiday – until everything begins to go horribly wrong . . .

Colin becomes aware of a ghastly stench of death and decay from the land . . . Prill is haunted by a fearsome skeleton-woman who crawls through her dreams in hideous torment . . . Baby Alison falls sick with a sinister illness . . .

And their cousin Oliver? In those stiflingly hot summer days, as some nameless evil from the past closes in on them, Oliver remains unnaturally, unnervingly calm . . .

Black Harvest was picked by schoolchildren to be included in their twenty-four best books in the "Children's Choice" British book promotion of 1984. One reader said: "It was like opening the door of a fridge . . ."

Ann Cheetham has written three further spinechilling novels featuring Oliver Wright and his cousins, Colin and Prill Blakeman: *The Beggar's Curse*, *The Witch of Lagg* and *The Pit*.

The Beggar's Curse

Ann Cheetham

Is there no escape from the village of evil?

When Colin, Prill and Oliver arrive in Stang they realize at once that something is wrong with the village. Up on the surrounding hills spring is blossoming, but in this dark little valley no flowers bloom and birds never sing.

Prill knows there is something sinister about the age-old rituals of the village play. Colin knows the gruesome incidents that keep happening are no accidents. But Oliver alone knows the awful secret of Stang and sees the ancient evil rising from the black waters of Blake's Pit. He feels the terrible power of the beggarman's curse.

The Beggar's Curse is a chilling sequel to *Black Harvest*. Ann Cheetham has written two further spinechilling novels, *The Witch of Lagg* and *The Pit*.

The Witch of Lagg

Neither Colin, Oliver nor Prill is looking forward to spending their holidays with gloomy Grierson of Lagg's Castle. They nickname the creepy mansion 'Castle Dracula' but the terrible secret it hides is more sinister and more complicated than that of a vampire. As the cousins explore the icy rooms and the dark woods, they find themselves victims of an ancient, evil and murderous force . . .

Other spinechilling novels by Ann Cheetham include:

Black Harvest
The Beggar's Curse
The Pit